T0196145

The Dead Lawyer Conspiracy II

THE
PANTHER
RESURRECTION

Jane T. Robe

iUniverse, Inc.
Bloomington

The Dead Lawyer Conspiracy II
The Panther Resurrection

iUniverse books may be ordered through booksellers or by contacting:

iUniverse
1663 Liberty Drive
Bloomington, IN 47403
www.iuniverse.com
1-800-Authors (1-800-288-4677)

ISBN: 978-1-4759-5742-6 (sc)
ISBN: 978-1-4759-5744-0 (hc)
ISBN: 978-1-4759-5743-3 (e)

Library of Congress Control Number: 2012922926

Printed in the United States of America

iUniverse rev. date: 12/17/2012

"INFORMATION IS THE CURRENCY OF DEMOCRACY."

Thomas Jefferson

PREFACE

The Panther Resurrection continues *The Dead Lawyer Conspiracy* and resumes the story of Rachel Ballentine and her unique cast of characters. Focusing on conspiracy theories revolving around today's global economic crisis and mistrust of the powerful elite, it probes the possibility of secret cabals plotting to rule the world. Adding the latest scientific advances and humanity's rising spiritual awareness, this volume may also have you examining more than you anticipated.

Since lawyers will be your main companions on this sojourn, I have also included a lawsuit raising first amendment issues recently presented to our courts.

Importantly, I give thanks and gratitude for the multitude of friends who have supported my writing and assisted me on this journey. Special recognition to Stefano Cassolato whose generosity has helped me to realize my literary dreams, Jan "K" Bixler for her close friendship and support, Mark Simon for his lifelong friendship, George Nedeff for his wisdom and erudite *Georgeisms*, Kathleen Shapona for reminding me everything in its right time, my financial guru and close friend Jerry, the wonderful authors in my San Francisco and P-Town writing groups who unfailingly offered their encouragement, my editor Patricia La Barbera, Marsha Garland, *Cuz* John, and Mr. Goshen, Mr. Godfrey, Angel, Eesan, Gabriel, and Jast, my beloved writing master.

And so, dear reader, I hope you enjoy the continuation of Rachel's story, and where it shall lead.

Regards,
Jane T. Robe

PROLOGUE

E veryone's attention focused on the meticulously dressed man seated at the head of the conference table. The slight tightening around his eyes and the flare of his nostrils indicated his fury. They'd lost a steady source of funds and compromised one of their operations.

Even though they'd covered their tracks, he'd want to ensure there would be no further digging. The man was thorough. He was vengeful as well—someone would have to pay.

"Exterminate. One of them has to go," the man finally decided. He then circled a face on the photo in front of him.

"Yes, sir," the subordinate on his right agreed, before quietly exiting. The four remaining operatives waited. The man tapped the knot of his crimson silk tie with his index finger and adjusted the cuff on his black suit, and asked, "Have you found it?"

Several shifted in their seats. All avoided his gaze. The seconds loudly ticked by.

"So the answer is no," the man concluded when no one spoke.

"Find it!" he harshly ordered into the stillness.

Knowing their lives depended on it, the operatives replied, "Yes, sir," as one, and quickly filed out of the room. The man then looked across the table at his son. "They will find it."

"Yes," his son confirmed.

"Whatever the cost," he coldly added.

An icy chill lingered in the air long after they'd left the room.

CHAPTER 1

"**C**an't you go any faster?"

"Rachel, for the third time, I'm going as fast as I can."

"Just go faster." I gripped the seat to keep my hands from shaking.

Ed stopped at the red light and turned toward me. He tucked a stray lock of dark hair behind my ear. "We'll be there in a minute," he said, and placed his hand on mine.

I nodded as tears coursed down my cheeks. When the light changed, I repeated, "Go faster." Ed squeezed my hand, and then shifted gears to get up the steep hill.

How could Oliver be shot? My mentor, my friend, it just couldn't be. My brain tried to wrap itself around the notion, but it wouldn't compute. *I would have felt it!* No, it was a mistake, I decided as Ed drove into the hospital lot and parked. We rushed to the emergency room entrance and followed the signs to the reception desk.

"Where's Oliver?" I stared at the clerk, not caring if I were rude.

"Oliver?" He wrinkled his forehead and looked at Ed.

"James Oliver Kendall. Gunshot wound."

"Are you a family member?"

"Well, no," Ed said.

"I am," I lied. "Now where is Oliver?"

He glanced at his computer screen. "Third floor. He's going into surgery."

I saw Phil when the elevator doors opened on the third floor, and I ran down the hallway. "What's going on?" I asked when I reached him. Short and wiry, his customary frenetic energy was absent, and he looked all of his seventy years.

Before he could answer, I heard, "Kiddo?"

Oliver lay on a gurney with tubes and equipment hooked up to him. Dried blood and gauze matted his narrow chest, and pain flooded his blue eyes. He seemed broken. I gently touched his hand, and then leaned down to kiss his cheek. Tears spilled down mine.

"Excuse me, miss, but we need to get him into surgery." One of the nurses tried to move me aside.

"You'll be fine. I love you, Oliver," I whispered as the attendants wheeled him through the operating room doors.

"Phil, what happened?" I asked. He was leaning against the wall looking sick.

"I don't know! We'd just had lunch downtown. We were walking back to the car and talking about my wife's plan to throw Oliver a seventieth birthday party. And then…"

"And then?"

"He had a red stain on his shirt and collapsed," Phil said, wringing his hands. "I know I called 911, and—"

"Okay, Phil," I said, feeling his distress. I led him to the vinyl chairs, and took a seat next to Ed. It was going to be a long wait.

I'd met Oliver, a prominent San Francisco attorney, almost three years ago, and we quickly became friends. He later hired me as an associate attorney at his prestigious law firm, and guided me through a huge case we'd named "The Dead Lawyer Conspiracy." Ed Brogan was the private investigator who'd worked with us on it. Tall, muscular, and in his late thirties, with a military-style buzz cut and intelligent dark eyes, he was now my fiancé.

"Who would want to hurt Oliver?" It just didn't make any sense.

"It's the dead lawyer case. It has to be," Phil said. He turned to Ed. "We'll all need security."

Three hours later a man in green scrubs walked over to the nurse's station. He was directed to our group.

"Oliver Kendall's family?"

"How is he?" I jumped up from my seat.

"I'm Dr. Rothman. The bullet nicked his lung and came close to his spine. There was a lot of internal bleeding. He's in ICU."

"Is he going to make it?" Phil asked.

The doctor shrugged and said, "We'll know more tomorrow," and walked away.

My heart sank. I didn't realize I was crying until Ed handed me a tissue. After wiping my face, I looked at Phil. "What do we do?"

"We find out who did this, and get them."

No, we destroy them.

CHAPTER 2

We got home around midnight, and I dropped into an exhausted sleep.

"Rachel, listen to me."

All I saw were diaphanous white clouds billowing around me, yet the voice…

"Is that you, Oliver?" I called out.

The clouds thinned, and I could see Oliver moving toward me. He lifted his arm and then reached out to touch me, but his hand felt ice cold.

I bolted awake in my bed.

What was that? Careful not to wake Ed, I moved the covers aside and padded down the hall toward my office. Shadows appeared on the gold walls when I switched on a lamp. Overstuffed bookcases filled the cramped space while legal texts, work files, and a myriad of framed photos littered my desk. Sitting, I picked up a picture and ran my index finger across the glass. Three beaming smiles stared back at me: Oliver, Phil, and me after the last Dead Lawyer Conspiracy court hearing.

Tears welled and slipped down my cheeks unheeded. It seemed so long ago that I'd met Oliver in Huntington Park, a tiny area at the top of Nob Hill with a small swing set in the center. I'd discovered the park while in law school and went there to unwind. It was a haven when waiting for my bar exam results.

One afternoon, I noticed a slight, elderly man with a crooked smile and twinkling blue eyes on a swing, and introduced myself. We struck up a conversation and then a friendship, and twilight at the swings with Oliver became one of my favorite pastimes. To think I might lose him… I felt my stomach tighten.

Oliver, a widower and retired partner at Acker & Kendall, a well-regarded law firm, had taken to walking over to Huntington Park to pass the time. He was brilliant, and he was bored. So when I told him about a case I'd stumbled across involving the state bar, he decided to hire me at his law firm and come out of retirement to mentor me through it. I enjoyed sharing Oliver's passion for history. I was always learning around him and liked how he called me *kiddo*. Oliver also had an enormous sweet tooth, and Mr. Chocolate and Mr. Cookie were his closest friends. But Oliver was my best friend.

When he'd later asked his sailing buddies, renowned litigators Phil Brown and Robert "RD" Dunkin, to join us on the case, I was nervous. Their prowess in the courtroom and arguments before the Supreme Court were legendary. Masters of their craft, these men treated me like their precocious daughter, and I loved them, these septuagenarians whom I'd fondly dubbed my personal *grey panthers*. Weary, I set the picture down and sighed. It was then I felt Ed's hand on my shoulder and leaned into it.

"You need to get some sleep, babe."

Nodding, I shut the light and extinguished the shadows.

We returned to the hospital a few hours later. With nothing to do but wait, I fell asleep again.

"Rachel, you have to remember," I heard Oliver shout as swirling white clouds moved around me.

"Oliver, where are you?" I yelled into the hazy white wall. And like magic, he appeared in front of me.

"What do I have to remember?" I asked.

"Here," he said and held out his hand.

I leaned in, and Oliver vanished.

My eyes popped open, and I burst upright in the waiting room chair, aware my heart was racing. I then walked over to the nurse's station and said I needed to see Oliver.

"He's still unconscious," the duty nurse said, busy making notes in a chart.

"It doesn't matter. I need to see him. Please, please, I have to," I begged.

She stopped and stared at me. I probably looked like a teenager instead of a successful attorney nearing thirty, with my long hair hastily pulled into a ponytail, and wearing a baggy sweatshirt and jeans. I felt my eyes fill with tears and repeated, "Please." She sighed and put the chart down.

Standing by Oliver's bedside, I gently touched his hand. It was cold. "Oliver, I know you're calling me. I can hear you. So, please wake up." I bent and kissed his cheek, unnerved by the hissing and clacking of the equipment in the room. I spotted Dr. Rothman speaking with Phil as I walked back down the hall.

"How is he?" I asked.

"Critical. He needs to wake up," the doctor said.

I nodded and sat down next to Ed and texted Oliver's son, James. He was out of the country, and I needed to send him an update on Oliver's condition. I then leaned into Ed, and we waited. Hours passed as I watched Phil's frantic march up and down the hallway. At nine, the doctor sent us home, promising to call if there were any changes.

I slept fitfully. Oliver kept waking me up, repeatedly yelling something I couldn't hear. It was frustrating. Some would say crazy, but I knew it was Oliver.

When we returned to the hospital the next morning, I was upset to learn he was still unconscious. Taking his hand, I whispered, "Oliver, I know you're trying to tell me something. Please, please just wake up and say it." I then took a seat next to his bed and started talking about times we'd shared. Dr. Rothman had said it might help.

When I recalled telling Oliver about my angels, I began to smile. It was the second day of law school, and I'd walked down the hill to attend class. Waiting at the corner of Market and Second Street for the crossing light to turn green, I heard the word *jump* loudly reverberate within my body as a feeling of warmth surrounded me. Without hesitation, I bent my knees and propelled myself as high up in the air as I could, at the very moment a car sped around the corner and jumped the curb. Midair, I'd rolled over the hood and landed on my butt in the street, winded and stunned, but unharmed as the car raced off.

Nearby witnesses ran to my aid, shocked when I shakily rose uninjured.

"Why'd you jump straight up?" a man helping me across the street asked.

"It saved your life," a woman added.

"Someone told me to jump," I said, still dazed.

"Your angels," the woman explained as I looked into her unusual green eyes.

"Yes, my angels," I agreed, and the downtown clock tower chimed.

This wasn't the first time I'd encountered my angels. I'd felt and heard them before. Yet looking back, I realized they didn't always help me or speak to me, and I couldn't find any logic or rules to explain when they did. So I let it go, accepting it was beyond my understanding, and felt thankful for the times I was open and in the right space to hear them.

Years later, I'd sat between Ed and Oliver at the swings in Huntington Park and shared my story while the sky darkened and the park worked its magic. Neither had spoken. They didn't have to. These men might not share my beliefs, but they allowed for them, and for that I was eternally grateful. And so I said, "Angels, please help Oliver," just as the nurse tapped me on the shoulder and told me it was time to leave.

That night, Oliver appeared in my dreams once again. Standing at the far end of a small cobblestone bridge, he started moving toward me.

"Rachel, you need to remember," Oliver shouted.

"Remember what?" I yelled back in frustration, walking toward him.

"Remember the key," he said, as we met in the middle of the bridge.

"The key?"

Oliver smiled. He glowed. Then he handed me a shiny gold key on a string and disappeared. The key glistened as bright white light enveloped me, and I felt peaceful. I awoke feeling rested and hopeful.

When we returned to the hospital, I let Oliver know. "I heard 'the key.' Now it's time to wake up."

After another night of nocturnal visits, I'd had it. "Okay Oliver," I said as soon as I entered the ICU that morning. "Enough is enough. Wake up! I need to get some sleep."

"I heard you. You don't need to yell," he whispered, and slowly opened his eyes.

"Oliver, you're back." Looking about, I shouted, "Nurse, nurse!"

The police officer guarding the ICU entrance rushed in. Several nurses followed. "He's awake," I explained as a nurse walked over to Oliver and checked his pulse. She then told me to leave.

"What? I need to talk to him," I said. But no amount of wheedling would change her mind, so I joined Ed in the hallway and filled him in. I then texted the others with the news.

Relief flooded the air while we waited for the doctor's update. Ten minutes later, he told us that Oliver's waking up was a good sign but warned that he wasn't out of the woods. With possible infection, high blood pressure, and Oliver's age, the recovery process would be long.

As I watched everyone somberly digest this information, deep feelings of gratitude washed over me. Looking up, I softly said, "Thank you." Sensations of warmth gently surrounded me as I heard *you're welcome* drift back in response.

"Did you just say you're welcome?" Ed asked, frowning.

Smiling, I shook my head no.

My angels have manners, after all.

CHAPTER 3

L ater that afternoon, I walked into my home office with dread. I'd never wanted to deal with this case again. I sat at my desk and pulled the large file from the back of the drawer. Taking a deep breath, I opened it. A case chronology was affixed to the top of The Dead Lawyer Conspiracy file, and my eyes moved down the page.

We'd discovered that every state's bar association had been overcharging attorney bar dues for years. The surplus money went to the two corporations providing substance abuse programs, and education programs for the nation's bar associations. While program fees had significantly increased over the years, corresponding services hadn't, leaving us wondering where the money went. With millions of attorneys paying overages of millions each year, it was going somewhere.

It wasn't exactly legal when Ed had Geoffrey, his computer whiz, hack into the two corporations and follow the money. He tracked millions going to a third corporation, who then transferred it to a Caribbean holding company. The same millions allegedly paid to fictitious employees using dead lawyers' identities, that is. Geoffrey then hacked into the holding company and started copying. Their system immediately shut down and locked Geoffrey out, though not before he'd copied a file containing a list of mercenaries and information on operations they'd worked on.

When a man on the list agreed to speak with us, discretion

was crucial, so Ed and I pretended to be on a romantic weekend getaway at a historic San Diego hotel as a cover for a meeting. After checking in, we'd set off on a leisurely stroll along the shore, soon stopping to sit on a bench and gaze at the view. A sweaty man wearing running gear had just plopped down next to us, seemingly to catch his breath, and whispered, "You're being tailed," when he was shot. I'd gone into shock, and completely freaked out.

Meanwhile, the two corporations' records were destroyed in a fire, the charred remains of their bookkeeper found in the rubble. Next, the three men comprising the corporations board of directors were killed in a car crash, and the attorney who'd set everything up committed suicide a week later. And then the Caribbean holding company vanished.

Deciding not to be foolish, we forwent investigating the San Diego man's murder. Instead, we got the hell out of Dodge once the bars reluctantly agreed to refund the overcharges. I'd closed the file and blocked San Diego from my mind. And for nearly a year, I had. Until now. I looked down and wiped my tears from the page.

"Rachel?" Ed said from the doorway, his voice filled with concern.

"I'm okay." I grabbed a tissue and closed the file. He then told me he'd asked everyone to meet us at Oliver's residence, and it was time to go upstairs. Occupying the top floor of a fifteen-story Nob Hill building, the penthouse measured nearly three thousand square feet and afforded expansive views of the city. I'd bought my small condo in the same building last year.

I was pacing in Oliver's entry hall when Phil and William stepped off the private elevator with their burly security details. Stout and over sixty, William Acker reminded me of Santa Claus and smelled like the peppermint hard candies that filled his pockets. He was also *the* Acker in the law firm of Acker & Kendall, and my boss.

His deep voice boomed, "Rachel," as he enveloped me in

a peppermint hug, and told me not to worry about work. My calendar had been cleared for the next two weeks.

Relieved, I said, "Thank you," and returned the hug.

The security then moved into the living room, an enormous space with floor-to-ceiling windows facing the bay, while Ed ushered us down the hall toward Oliver's den. Oversized black leather sofas and matching reclining chairs provided plenty of seating. William settled his large frame into a chair and rubbed his balding pate, before telling us he'd gone through Oliver's case files for the last twenty years and found zilch.

"It's the dead lawyer case." Phil frantically paced and jingled the coins in his pockets.

"Nothing else makes sense," William agreed with a heavy sigh punctuated by the crinkling sound of a candy wrapper.

"But why? The police said Oliver was shot by a professional with a high-powered rifle, so it had to be for a reason. So what was it?" I asked.

"Revenge or they're warning us not to investigate further," Phil said.

"Investigate what further?" I jumped up, my hands clenched into fists at my sides.

"Rachel," Ed whispered, placing his hand on my arm.

"Sorry." I needed to think and not react. Okay, so if it was a warning to stay away, what could they be telling us to stay away from? I wondered as Ed told us he'd arranged security for RD. The distinguished attorney had retired and moved to Denver after the dead lawyer case ended. Ed then detailed his efforts to find the sniper, from tracing the bullet to collecting surveillance video based on the shot's trajectory. He'd also enlisted the help of all of his contacts. As a former San Francisco police officer, he had many.

William frowned and opened another candy. "I don't know, maybe we should leave this for the police?"

I stared at him. Phil stopped pacing and looked at him as if he'd grown a second head.

"William, we can't! If we wait for the police to figure it out, one of us could get killed," I said.

"Right. And I'm not sitting around doing nothing," Phil declared. He resumed pacing and jingling the coins in his pockets. "What was the body count at the end of the case?"

"Six. The bookkeeper, the attorney, and the three board members. And then there was the San Diego man," I answered.

"He never fit. He wasn't connected to the corporations," Phil said.

I realized he was right. "What do we know about him?"

"The police files only identified him as John Doe, and he worked as a mercenary under the alias John Done. That's it." Ed shrugged.

Something nudged at my memory just out of reach. "I think we're missing something."

"Fine, why don't we all get some sleep and talk again tomorrow?" Phil asked.

Ed and I were riding downstairs in the elevator when I told him I needed to say something.

"Should I be worried?"

"No. I just wanted to say thank you for being here for me."

"I love you." Ed squeezed my hand.

"I know." I hugged him tightly just as the door opened at our floor.

"Angels, thank you for him too," I later whispered when we went to bed.

"Did you say you're welcome again?" Ed mumbled into his pillow, before falling asleep.

Smiling, I snuggled closer.

• • •

"I need to walk the labyrinth," I told Ed the next morning.

"Not without me! It's not safe."

An hour later we walked the three blocks to Grace Cathedral. I'd discovered the cathedral's labyrinths, an indoor wool tapestry carpet and an outdoor one made of terrazzo stone, shortly after I'd started law school, and had found them a welcome reprieve from the academic stress. Years later, I still used them as a tool to help me find peace and unlock the answers within.

Even though the labyrinth was a circuitous pattern with many twists and turns, it had only one path. You walked one way and returned the same way. You started by trying to empty your mind and listen to your breath. During the walk to the center, people let go of random thoughts and distractions in order to quiet their minds. Once you reached the center, you could stay there to meditate and pray and receive whatever illumination you could. Finally, you went back along the same path you came.

And so I returned to where I'd started on the carpet and looked at Ed and asked, "Where's the key?"

"Huh?"

"You know, the key you took from the dead guy in San Diego when you checked for a pulse," I explained. It looked like a regular gold house key worn on a string around the man's neck, and we'd never figured out what it opened. It's what Oliver had been telling me, and I'd forgotten about it before walking the labyrinth.

"Oh, that key. It's in my office safe."

"We need to get it."

"Why?"

I stared at him in response.

Ed sighed, muttered, "Fine, whatever," and we left.

Thirty minutes later we stood in his downtown office and he handed me what looked like an ordinary shiny gold house key. Closing my fingers around it, I shut my eyes, and let the answers come. When I felt Ed tap me on the shoulder, I opened my eyes.

"This is why," I said as flashes of Oliver handing me the key surfaced along with the unblinking stare of the San Diego man lying on the ground with his blood pooling around him.

"What is why?"

"Could you have someone examine this?"

"Examine the key?"

"Like under a microscope?"

"Microscope?"

"Ed, you're repeating what I say. We never had a professional examine the key to see if it was more than just a normal house key. We only looked for what a regular key would open, and forgot about it when we closed the dead lawyer case."

Ed took the key and stared at it, before flipping it over several times.

"I think, no, I know there is something on that key," I added.

"You know?" He looked up.

"Yes, I know."

"How could you?"

"Well ..."

"Well?" Ed questioned.

"Okay, but you asked." At his nod I continued. "When Oliver was unconscious he kept visiting me in my sleep. He'd call out to me and wake me up. It was driving me crazy because I knew he was telling me something, I just couldn't recall it. And then he started yelling at me to remember. It wasn't until the day before he woke up that I really heard him. He said to remember the key, and then he handed me a gold key on a string. Just like that one," I said, pointing at his hand.

"Oliver spoke to you while he was unconscious," Ed said, and raised his brows, "And while you were dreaming."

"Yes, he did." I stared him straight in the eye.

"I know you two have a special bond, but that ..." A moment later he shrugged and said, "Okay."

"Just okay?"

"Yes, I believe you, so just okay."

"Thanks for not telling me I'm crazy."

"You are crazy, but I'm getting used to it... I think." Ed brushed my long hair away from my face and kissed me softly. Bemused, I watched him pocket the key, then phone someone.

"Your microscope guy?" I asked when he hung up.

Ed nodded.

"Do you have a guy for everything?"

"Probably."

CHAPTER 4

We drove toward San Francisco's Fisherman's Wharf to meet Ed's guy. At its southeast end stood Pier 39, a tourist shopping bonanza hiding a city treasure— hundreds of sea lions. Years ago they took over the adjacent boat marina to lazily bask and sun bathe on the empty slip moorings, and bark, yes bark, among themselves. It's one of my favorite places, and I asked Ed if we could go there after seeing his guy.

"Don't you ever get sick of them?"

Watching the sea lions lie in the sun, seemingly without a care, calmed me. So I shook my head, and then smiled, recalling the first time Oliver and I had walked down to the pier. He'd bet I didn't know the difference between a sea lion and a seal. How was I supposed to know that sea lions had ears and seals didn't? The wager had cost me two plastic souvenir jackets with the city's name emblazoned on the back.

At Ed's inquiring look, I explained.

"So that's why you have that tacky thing. Don't worry, you'll be having fun with Oliver again before you know it." Ed turned off the engine.

He'd parked in front of a book store. Odd, I thought, and followed him inside. I immediately smelled the heavenly aroma of coffee, and slowed. I'm a coffee addict and proud of it.

"When we leave," Ed said, without stopping

I nodded and trailed him to the escalator. Once upstairs, he took my hand and led me toward the mystery section. I raised one eyebrow in question.

"Did you notice my eyebrow?" I whispered.

"Yes, Rachel, I noticed your eyebrow."

"Uncle Pete taught me."

"Uncle Pete," Ed said, with a wry smile.

A moment later, Ed and I stopped beside a woman arranging a book display.

She looked up when we approached. "May I help you?"

"Actually, yes. We're looking for these books." Ed handed her a sheet of paper he pulled out of his pocket.

Books? We were supposed to be meeting his guy.

The woman smiled. "You're in the wrong section. This way."

We followed her to an area on the right.

"Here's the first one, but I'll need to check in the stockroom for the others. I'll be back in a few minutes."

Ed picked up a book and idly flipped through it.

What was going on? And then I knew. She was his "guy." He must have given her the key when he gave her the page.

She came back about ten minutes later. "Sorry, we're out of them. I thought, well…" She returned Ed's list.

"No worries." He pocketed the list. "I'll order them online, and thanks."

She winked and turned to help another customer.

"Let's pay for this, get your coffee fix, and go see the lions." Ed led me toward the escalator.

Purchases in hand, we returned to his car and drove the few short blocks to the Pier 39 parking lot. On the walk over I asked what was going on.

"That was Ruth."

"And?"

He handed me the page. It read "Microchip embedded. Forensic analysis of data needed—likely encoded."

"What? That's incredible." I stared at the words. "It really is the key."

"Yes, let's go." Ed took the page and steered me toward the pier.

My mind was still turning over what could possibly be on the chip when we reached the sea lions. There were rows of them and almost no tourists—perfect. Ed and I leaned against the wooden rail and stood watching the lions, and the setting sun. At least I thought we were until I noticed Ed's careful surveillance of the area.

"What's wrong?"

"Nothing, babe." He nodded.

"Ed?"

"Two of my security team are trailing us."

I shivered. I'd been pretending things were back to normal. Scared, I took Ed's hand and moved closer. A few minutes later we walked back to his jeep and headed home. Ed's house, that is. He owned one of the boxy pastel houses constructed in abundance just north of Golden Gate Park after World War II.

Seated in a large brown club chair in Ed's den, I asked, "So what do we do now?"

"Ruth's a forensic scientist and can spot things in places they shouldn't be. Now that we're sure there's a chip, we need a forensic computer analyst."

"What's a forensic scientist doing working in a book store?"

"Meeting with clients."

Great cover. I also realized that Oliver had been shot only five days ago, yet it seemed like years.

Ed phoned John Smith and suggested he join us for dinner. An ex-FBI agent in his midforties, he'd assisted us in the past. Straightforward and knowledgeable, he possessed an inner strength and integrity, and I liked him. When he arrived at eight, his six-foot-two muscular frame hidden under loose nondescript brown clothing, I smiled. I'd once asked him why he dressed like that, and he said it made him seem harmless. He was wrong. He was like Ed, too much testosterone to ignore.

Over mouth-watering lasagna, Ed and John discussed the police files and security footage they'd recovered. I learned the sniper shot Oliver with a M110 rifle from the roof of a building a half block away and the surveillance videos hadn't helped identify the shooter. When Ed handed the key to John and asked him to give it to Dr. Feden, I said, "Doctor who?"

"Dr. Feden. He's a computer encryption expert." Ed warned it might be weeks before we knew anything.

Weeks, I thought with dismay. Our only real lead, and there was nothing I could do but *wait*—that foul four-letter word. Didn't people understand? Sitting still frightened me. It made me feel helpless. I need to do something. There just had to be something. And then I looked across the table at John's rough-hewn features, and smiled. The universe was forever trying to teach me patience, but maybe if I helped John, the good karma might speed the cosmos up.

"Hey, John, are you dating anyone?" I broke into their conversation.

Silence reigned. He looked at Ed before saying "No," slowly.

"Why not?" I knew he'd split up with his girlfriend six months ago.

"I haven't met anyone," he said, and I couldn't tell if he was looking at me with fear or suspicion.

"Want me to fix you up? I know lots of people. What are you looking for?"

John bolted to his feet. "This was great, but I need to leave if I'm to hand over the key." He was gone two minutes later.

"John left pretty quickly," I said, pushing the food around on my plate. I speared a bite of lasagna, sniffed it, and set my fork down.

"Rachel, what's going on?" Ed stared at me.

"What?"

"You heard me. What's going on?" He sat next to me, and I felt the tears start to well. I looked down. Ed lifted my chin with his finger so I couldn't look away.

"I'm scared," I blurted. "You said it could take weeks. What if they hurt one of us while we're doing nothing and just waiting?"

Ed wrapped his arms around me. "It's okay. We don't need to know everything now. We will when we have to."

I moved closer and hoped he was right.

CHAPTER 5

"**H**i, kiddo," Oliver greeted when I walked into the ICU the following afternoon.

"Hey, Oliver."

He still looked extremely pale, and I knew there were bandages taped to his chest under his gown. Leaning down, I kissed his cheek then pulled a chair over and took a seat next to his bed. The cop and Ed's security man stood guard near the door.

"I hear they're moving you out of ICU tomorrow." I smiled. When Oliver didn't respond, I touched his arm. "What's up, Oliver?"

"I want to tell you something." He seemed serious.

"Shoot."

Oliver winced.

"Oops, sorry. What do you want to tell me?"

"Well." He paused. "When I was unconscious, I had these dreams, and since you like this sort of thing…"

"Yes, Oliver?"

"And …"

"Oliver, I heard you."

"You did?" Oliver's voice rose.

Warmth surrounded me and I smiled. "Yes, Oliver, I heard you. And why don't we talk about this after they move you?"

"Yes," he agreed as a nurse walked in, signaling my time was up.

• • •

The next day Ed handed me a folder.

"What's this?"

"The key."

I opened the file and saw a series of snapshots at different magnifications. Each enlargement increased the resolution of the chip embedded in the key's surface. Next came photographs of the removed chip, followed by several pages of what I presumed was encrypted data. It looked like gibberish to me. The last pictures showed a sequence of enlargements of the key's other side. A few small scratches on the shaft, when magnified, appeared elliptical and forming an eight. How strange.

"Dr. Feden, my computer guy, is working on deciphering it," Ed said.

I nodded and flipped through the pages once again. "How long until we know what this means?"

"No idea. Remember, I said it could take weeks."

"So we have to wait?"

"Yes, Rachel, we have to wait."

"I truly hate that four-letter word," I said, not for the first time.

• • •

Ed arranged a meeting at Oliver's penthouse that same evening. Phil and William showed up with their bodyguards in tow. The security remained in the entry hall, and we moved into the den. Once everyone was seated, Ed filled them in on what we knew about the shooter. He then told them about the microchip concealed in the key.

"A microchip? How'd you know to look for it?" Phil asked.

Ed turned and looked at me. About to gloss over it, I decided instead they should know. "Okay, well, just open your minds to this," I prefaced, and recounted what I'd experienced while Oliver was unconscious.

"You're kidding, right?" Phil said.

When I shook my head, they looked at each other.

"You're saying that Oliver spoke to you while you were sleeping," William said, furrowing his brow.

"Yes."

"Don't you think it's more likely that the key was in the back of your mind already, and you were just dreaming?" Phil asked.

"No."

"Rachel, we all know how close you and Oliver are. You were upset and hardly sleeping, and maybe…confused," William said, unwrapping a candy.

"No." I stared at the floor.

"Well, anything's possible," Phil said, and I looked up. "Besides, who cares how we discovered it? What's on the microchip?" Phil jingled the coins in his pockets.

Just like Phil to cut to the chase, I thought as Ed told them what we knew about the chip. He also said he doubted anyone knew he took the key since someone would have tried to get it back already if they did.

"Which is why I'm not discarding the idea of revenge. This came in today's mail," Phil said, and reached inside his jacket breast pocket to pull out an envelope. His hand shook as he removed a single sheet of white paper, and laid it on the coffee table. **YOUR NEXT** screamed up at us in large black capital letters. My body started to tremble.

"Well, they're not that smart. They can't spell," Phil said, after a moment.

"Not the time, Phil." My hands clenched into fists and tears beckoned. The idea that someone would shoot Oliver simply to get even with us was terrifying. The fact that they might do it again to any of us, at any time, was petrifying.

"I think you should retire Phil," William said. "You and Oliver were the lead attorneys on the case. Maybe they'll back off if they think you're giving up."

"I am *not* retiring," Phil said, pulling his bow tie askew and crossing his thin arms in front of him.

"Why not?" William asked.

"If you retire, you're old," Phil said, his nasally voice practically squeaking.

I was so tense I couldn't help it. I giggled, and then laughed.

"Are you done?"

"Yes, Phil," I said, feeling better.

Ed suggested we wait and see what his computer guy found. If we knew what we were dealing with, we could better decide what to do. In the meantime, we'd tell the police about the note.

"Fine. And I'll talk to Pete and have him look into the San Diego man," Phil said. Peter Simpson, septuagenarian news anchor and media legend, was a close friend of Phil's and an invaluable resource.

Heading downstairs, I asked Ed whether I should buy Phil a watch to celebrate his retirement. "They always give people a watch when they retire. It'll make it look authentic."

"Not buying it, Rachel. You enjoy teasing him."

"Well, maybe a little."

CHAPTER 6

I was sitting in a chair next to Oliver's hospital bed, editing a contract and munching on a cookie. Oliver had been transferred out of ICU almost a week ago, and he was rapidly improving. His color was returning, and Dr. Rothman had him walking around. I knew he was better when he asked me to bring him cookies.

"Energy food for the brain with potent healing qualities," he'd argued.

Reaching over, I grabbed another cookie from the nightstand and kept reading.

"I need to have a talk with you," Oliver blurted, and I looked up. I hadn't noticed him wake.

"Okay, Oliver, talk." I put the document down.

"Well, you remember when I told you I'd been dreaming while I was unconscious?"

"Yes," I said nodding, having waited for him to bring this up again. Oliver hated being pushed or rushed, and if I'd pressed, he would have clammed up.

"Well, I don't think I was dreaming."

"Not dreaming?"

"No, not dreaming," Oliver confirmed.

"Why's that?"

"I could see people coming in and out of my room, and I could also hear them."

"Is that so?"

"Yes, and I could see me. It was like I was looking down, and I could see myself sleeping in this bed with all these machines around me. I kept calling out, but no one heard. That is, except you."

I smiled. "Yes, Oliver I heard you. You wouldn't let me sleep."

"What did you hear?"

"Well, it wasn't really heard. I'd go to sleep and wake up knowing you were calling to me."

"Really?" Oliver said, his voice rising.

"Yes, really. One time I heard you say 'remember the key' and then you handed me a gold key on a string."

That seemed to startle him. "I thought I imagined that. It didn't make sense."

"It made a lot of sense once I thought about it. Remember the key Ed took from the man who was killed in San Diego?"

"Oh, yeah, I forgot about that."

"So did I. But above all it made me sure that we're connected, and in a way that's absolutely incredible."

"Really?" he asked again.

"Yep," I said as Dr. Rothman entered the room, and then tapped his watch to signal the end of my visit. "Times up. See ya later alligator." I bent and kissed his cheek.

"Okay, but I want to talk more about this."

"Sure, Oliver," I agreed, and left. Who'd have figured? It was only a short time ago I was trying to convince him that we'd known each other in a prior life and were destined to meet, and here he was talking about an out-of-body experience.

"What are you smiling about?" Ed asked when I joined him.

"Oliver. How the universe works."

"What do you mean?"

"Our worst experiences are also our greatest teachers. If you pay attention, your mind can open to all sorts of possibilities."

"Oliver?"

"Wide open."

• • •

Ed and I visited Oliver at the hospital every day. As we approached his room one time I heard Phil ask, "Remember when he color coded all the documents and files on the bank case, and we couldn't find anything?"

"How could I forget?" William answered. "He made us crazy until he made that index, tan for tax records and magenta for money. Who does that?"

"He did the same thing on the dead lawyer case," I said as Ed and I walked in. Bouquets of flowers and cards sat on every available space.

"I'm organized," Oliver defended.

"You're nuts," Phil said, and everyone laughed.

Oliver's doctor had told him he could go home in a few days, and no amount of teasing could dim his smile. He was overjoyed. I was both thrilled and scared by the news.

"Hey guys, there's something that's been bothering me." I waited to gain everyone's attention. "If the shooter's goal was to kill Oliver, do you think he'll try again?" The room grew very quiet.

"It's possible," Phil said.

"Then Oliver needs to die."

"What?" Oliver said, glaring at me.

"Well, not for real. I've watched gazillions of cop shows, and they always flush out the bad guys by watching who shows up at the funeral. We could pretend you died and hold a funeral."

"No!"

"It's only pretend, Oliver."

"I don't care. I came too close. No!"

"Well, we have to do something. They could try again," I warned. "How about a setback? We'll tell everyone you lapsed into a coma and were transferred to a private facility."

"But I'll really go home?"

We all nodded yes, and Oliver agreed.

Three days later, Ed and I sat inside a dark-blue van staring at his laptop screen. Two in the morning and pitch black outside. Moments ago, Geoffrey, Ed's computer whiz, had hacked into the hospital's mainframe and frozen their security camera feed so John could secretly collect Oliver and bring him downstairs. John, disguised with oversized horn-rim glasses and baggy blue scrubs, had a video camera attached to a small pendant around his neck.

We watched him push Oliver down the corridor in a wheelchair and into a nearby elevator. When the doors opened on the ground floor, John wheeled Oliver down the deserted hall. He then took Oliver's arm and helped him stand, and they walked out the side door where Ed and I waited.

"Piece of cake," John said, as we drove off into the night.

• • •

Oliver returned home almost three weeks after he'd been shot. When the penthouse elevator doors opened, Oliver beamed. A gigantic Welcome Home banner and multicolored helium balloons greeted him.

Oliver's smile said it all.

CHAPTER 7

As my boss, William had arranged for my calendar to be cleared and most of my cases reassigned, yet I still spent the following morning at home in my office returning work-related phone calls and responding to e-mail so that I didn't go upstairs to visit Oliver until lunchtime. When I walked into Oliver's bedroom, it felt like a coffin. The navy silk drapes were drawn. The lights dimmed. The defeated sighs coming from Oliver huddled under the damask quilt on his king-sized bed, the only sounds.

I sat on a brown-striped Bergere chair next to his bed. "What's wrong, Oliver?"

"You mean aside from getting shot?"

"You were so happy yesterday."

"To get out of the hospital. But now..."

"But now what?"

"But now I have to think." He sat up. "Someone shot me." He tapped his chest and winced. "Someone really tried to kill me. And I can't leave my home because they may try again. I'm a prisoner."

"It's only until we figure out what's going on. Why don't I open the curtains?" I stood and moved toward the windows.

"Stop!" Oliver yelled. I froze.

"What?" I asked as Wayne, Oliver's muscular bodyguard, ran in with his gun drawn. He scanned the dark room.

"It's okay, Wayne. Oliver was just telling me not to open the curtains." My heart was racing, and I stared at the gun, trying to remain calm.

"They can't shoot me if they can't see me. Don't open them," he pleaded in a panic.

"Okay, Oliver." I sat back down, feeling his terror even if I couldn't see it.

• • •

Oliver's home was a tomb when I returned the next morning. From the entry hall I saw the closed living and dining room drapes, and the air felt still.

"It's so dark in here, Wayne."

"Mr. Kendall wants it like this," he responded with a light southern drawl from his post by the elevator. A handsome six-foot black man with a history of military training, he'd keep Oliver safe.

I walked into Oliver's bedroom. "All the curtains are drawn." He huddled under the covers, a tray of untouched food near the foot of his bed.

"It's safer."

"I see. How about a lap around the apartment? Dr. Rothman said walking was good for you."

"No."

"Want me to turn on the TV or get you the newspaper?"

"No."

"Fine, I'll just sit with you."

"No, Rachel. I just want to rest and be alone."

"Are you sure?"

"Yes. Go home."

"Okay, Oliver," I said, leaving.

Oliver wasn't any better the next day. When I returned downstairs, I found Ed reading a few files at the kitchen table. The room, painted a sunny yellow with bright-white cabinets usually cheered me. It didn't now.

"What's up?" Ed asked, looking concerned.

"Oliver's depressed." I poured a mug of coffee and sat down beside him.

"He's only been home for a few days. Give it some time."

"Ed, you don't understand. He's really scared." I told him about the drawn curtains. Ed said he knew a guy who installed films over window glass that prevented anyone from seeing in, but you could still see out.

Of course he did.

An idea surfaced while Ed spoke on the phone to his guy. I later went online and purchased everything we'd need, and spent the next day convincing Ed to help. By the time the entire order was delivered the following afternoon, he was on board. Once Oliver was asleep, we brought the boxes and supplies upstairs and set to work.

The following morning, Ed and I went to visit Oliver. Wayne greeted us at the elevator, and told us the patient was awake.

"Morning," I said, walking into Oliver's bedroom. He was sitting up in bed.

"Hi, kiddo. Ed, thanks for having the window film installed yesterday."

"No problem."

"We have a surprise for you," I teased.

"A surprise?" Oliver didn't seem interested.

"Yeah, but you have to come with us and put this on."

Oliver looked at the black eye mask dangling from my fingers. As soon as he said okay, I helped him slip on his robe and the mask and led him down the hallway. When we reached the living room, I stopped and shouted, "Surprise!" Oliver pulled off the mask.

"What the…" And then he started laughing. In front of him was a swing set sitting atop a large sand box. Thick rubber mats lay beneath, completely hidden from view.

"I love it." Smiling, Oliver walked over and carefully sat down on a swing.

"Thought so," I murmured, and went to join him.

• • •

"Hey, there," I said, joining Oliver for a sunset swing later that day. It was still daylight, and sunshine streamed in the windows.

"Hi, kiddo."

"What're you thinking about?" I asked pushing off.

"Life. How quickly it passes."

"Oliver, you're only seventy."

"A lot of years."

"Should I get a sign for the doorway proclaiming this Oliver Kendall Park?"

"I don't believe we're appropriately zoned."

"Hey, that was really funny, Oliver. I just thought…"

"Necessity is the mother of invention."

"Yes, it is. Who said that?"

"Plato."

"Really?"

"Socrates said the unexamined life is not worth living," Oliver added, and I stared at him.

Okay, something was going on. "What's wrong, Oliver?" I stopped my swing.

"Nothing's wrong. Getting shot forced me to look at my life, that's all."

"I see. And?"

"And I've been remembering," Oliver said. "I was lying on the ground, and I couldn't move. Everything hurt, but there was this warm feeling around me. It was strange, almost comforting."

"Our angels. They were helping you."

"Really? I know you believe in angels, but…"

"Think about it." I resumed swinging, knowing not to push him.

"When I start falling asleep, I feel this horrible pain in my chest, and I can't breathe… I'm afraid to sleep," Oliver blurted minutes later.

I stopped my swing again. "You're safe now. No one's going to hurt you." But even as I said it, I wondered if it were true.

CHAPTER 8

As soon as I returned downstairs, Ed told me Dr. Feden had broken the encryption on the microchip. We were meeting him at Ed's place at eight. On the drive over, I asked Ed how he knew Dr. Feden. He strummed his fingers on the steering wheel, then paused before saying the doctor had made a lot of money on a number of global patents that some people wanted.

"We met when they kidnapped his daughter to convince him to sell them."

"What?"

"Let's just say John and I persuaded them otherwise."

His face grew dark, and I knew not to ask for details. Instead I said, "She's safe?" Ed nodded, and the topic dropped.

Shortly after eight, Ed walked into his den with a preppy-looking olive-skinned man in his midforties. "Dr. George Feden, my fiancé, Rachel Ballentine."

"Hello. I'm anxious to know what you found."

He returned my greeting, sat in one of the brown club chairs, and placed his briefcase on his lap. Ed and I took a seat on the chocolate leather sofa facing him. He opened his briefcase and took out the key.

"It's a copy. I made a mold of the key you gave me, before removing the microchip. You never know…" He shrugged. I picked up the key and stared at it, but didn't feel anything. When

Dr. Feden asked, "Have you ever heard of steganography?" I looked up.

"Steak and what?"

"Steganography," he repeated. He then told us it was the science of concealing messages, unlike cryptology, which was the art of encrypting a message to protect its contents. Steganography was used to hide the fact that there even was a message, and was commonly used to conceal information within computer files.

"So what did you find?" I asked.

"A great deal. It took a while to break the chip's data encryption, but once I did, I found this." He reached into his briefcase and handed us a few sheets of paper. The pages showed several black-and-white pictures of a wooded area, and a letter saying the place might be a good site for a new factory along with construction and manufacturing details.

"Any idea where this is?" Ed tapped the photos.

"No, but that's just the surface. We already knew there was an encrypted message, so I looked for a concealed one. Since digital pictures contain large amounts of data—bits—they're an easier and effective way to disguise messages." He paused. "Or other pictures."

The doctor had my attention. "Other pictures?"

"Yes. I won't bore you with the details, but they removed the last two bits of each color component resulting in the black-and-white photos you saw, so I went through the process of restoring them. Here's what I found." He then pulled a file from his briefcase and gave us another set of pictures. I stared at a picture of a coin and engraving diagrams, and my stomach tightened.

Dr. Feden cleared his throat and explained that the letter also concealed encrypted data. The stegotext—the plain words of the letter—contained details of the plant construction and manufacturing possibilities. But this plain text was itself encoded and hid information about cargo movements. Dr. Feden handed Ed a sheet with the deciphered text.

"Do we know what the cargo is?" Ed asked.

"My guess would be this coin. As for the location?" He ended with a shrug.

"Dr. Feden, thank you." Finally, something to go on.

"Great work," Ed added.

"For you, or John, anything. I can never repay you two," I overheard Dr. Feden say as Ed showed him out. While he was gone, I called Phil and arranged a meeting for tomorrow afternoon.

"I can't wait to share all this," I said, when Ed returned, and waved at the pictures on the coffee table. "It's incredible. I just wish we knew what it all meant."

"So do I. There's a connection somewhere."

"I bet it's whatever the San Diego man was involved in last year. Someone wanted us too scared to look into the guy."

"You could be right, and that might explain Oliver's shooting, but not why the San Diego man was shot," Ed said.

"Well, maybe he was hired to do something with the coin."

"And people were after him to get it?" Ed asked.

"Or maybe he stole the information and put it on the microchip?"

"Or did he steal the microchip and put it on the key?"

"Or steal the key which already had the chip?" I countered.

"This is giving me a headache," Ed muttered. "I need to think."

I said, "Fine," as he reached into the media cabinet and pulled out his favorite *Star Wars* videos. Ed was a big fan of the original trilogy and used them to focus and think. I waited while he started the movie, noting 'Arty' in the corner of the room, a two-foot-high droid robot who was interactive and responded to voice commands. We all had our quirks. I was an avid Trekkie. When Ed joined me on the sofa, I snuggled into his side.

Please keep us safe from the dark side, I prayed as the movie began.

• • •

At 1:15 p.m. I walked into Oliver's den and found Phil, William, and Oliver seated around a poker table set in the center of the room. Each had a stack of bills in front of them and beverages. A cart with sandwiches and snacks stood nearby. I was happy to see Oliver dressed in his normal weekend garb of chinos, cotton sweater, and topsiders, instead of his bathrobe.

"You're late," Phil said, shuffling a deck of cards.

"You'll forgive me once I tell you what Ed's computer guy shared last night," I said, holding up a file.

"Fine, sit. Five dollars to start ante up," Phil said.

For such rich guys, they took this all so seriously. I pulled the eighty-five dollars I had with me out of my pocket and took the remaining seat.

"Now, what did you find out?" William said, unwrapping a peppermint candy. So I told them about Dr. Feden breaking the encryption on the chip, and the first set of pictures. I slipped copies from the file and passed them around.

"A factory? What's so important about a factory?" Oliver asked.

"Nothing I can see, but Ed's looking into it." I then explained about steganography and how Dr. Feden found a second set of pictures hidden in the first ones.

"You're kidding," Phil said, and dealt. I glanced at my cards and sat still. Pictures of other hands popped into my head. Mentally shrugging, I set the cards down and pulled copies of the second set of pictures from the file and handed them out. The room grew very quiet.

"That's a coin. I don't recognize it," William said.

"And those are engraving schematics—what the hell did we get involved in?" Phil asked.

"Wish I knew. Someone went to a lot of trouble hiding the picture of the coin, but maybe it's a red herring. There are too many unknowns right now." I shrugged.

"Pete needed a few more days. He'll be here on Wednesday with whatever he's dug up on the San Diego man. My place around six," Phil said. He threw a twenty-dollar bill in the pot, and everyone added twenty more.

"Does anyone have any ideas or see a connection?" William asked, setting the images down and picking up his cards. A picture of two eights popped into my mind. I shook my head to clear it, and discarded two cards.

"There've been rumors of a new currency, like the euro, but combining the Americas, Canada, and Mexico. It's just a guess. Let's wait for Pete," Phil said, and dealt me two cards. Once everyone's cards were exchanged, Phil went clockwise around the table asking for bets. No one bet, and Phil tossed another twenty in the pot. Everyone folded except me. A picture of a hand with a two, three, seven, jack, and queen flashed in my head.

"I'll see your twenty and raise you twenty."

"I'll see your twenty and raise you twenty more," Phil said, staring at me, daring me to call.

His cockiness would work on a lot of folks, but not me. He was bluffing, so I tossed my last twenty dollars into the pot. "Call, two pair, jacks up."

Phil snapped his cards together facedown and scowled. "It's yours."

I couldn't help smiling and glanced at Oliver. He was staring at me. An hour later I'd cleaned them out.

"You're a shark," Oliver said, eyeing my winnings.

"No girls allowed anymore. You're banned," Phil added, and William seconded him.

"Sore losers," I muttered, stuffing the money into my bra, and left.

"What did they say?" Ed asked when I wandered into my kitchen shortly thereafter. He'd stayed behind to catch up on work.

"They won't play with me anymore."

"No, what'd they say about the microchip?"

I glared at him.

"Sorry, I'll play with you." He wiggled his brows.

"Thanks a bunch." Sighing, I pulled out the wad of bills and dropped them on the table. Ed's eyed widened. "Eight hundred and eleven dollars," I said, sitting.

"How'd that happen? I thought it was a friendly poker game."

"I think I may have cheated. I kept seeing pictures of their cards in my head."

"Do they know?"

"Only Oliver, and he thinks I'm crazy. But it's still his fault! He called me a shark, and they said I was banned."

Ed picked up the money. "We should go to Vegas."

"Ed, the karma."

"Just a thought. So what did they say?"

"They were surprised, but not shocked, and Phil said there've been rumors of an American version of the euro."

"And since we found schematics for a coin on the microchip…"

"Exactly. William suggested we talk to an economist. Do you have an economist guy? Forget it, silly question."

"I'll call her later. But right now I think it's time for me to play with you," he said.

"Strip poker?"

"That'll work."

•   •   •

We'd just turned in for the evening when I told Ed I was going into the office tomorrow.

"Couldn't you keep working from home? It's safer."

"No. Besides, there are security cameras and a guard posted in the lobby. I'll be safe."

"Rachel, we still don't know why Oliver was shot. Whoever did it might try again," he said, wearing a mulish expression. He crossed his arms in front of him.

"Ed, I need to." The silence grew uncomfortable, and I picked at the covers.

"Fine, I'll drive you in the morning," he finally said, and turned out the light.

CHAPTER 9

The following morning Ed stopped his jeep in front of Acker & Kendall's downtown office and reached behind his seat. "Inside, all day." He handed me my leather briefcase. I nodded and kissed him goodbye, then rushed toward the building's lobby.

Acker & Kendall occupied the entire fourth floor, which was shaped like a rectangle with six smaller offices on the three perimeter walls, and a large partner office in each corner. The fourth side was the lobby and reception area. The center of the rectangle housed a conference room, law library, and copier room, as well as the secretary and paralegal area.

It was a little after eight when I stepped off the elevator and walked into the law firm's elegant lobby decorated in muted golds, wines, and greens with dark-wood furnishings.

"Welcome back," the receptionist greeted and asked how Oliver was doing.

We spoke for a moment, and then I headed down the hall toward my office. Walking inside, I switched on the light and placed my briefcase on the cherry wood desk, and looked about. It had been awhile. Closing the door, I glanced in the full-length mirror. My green eyes had taken on my navy suit's blue hue. I also noticed the ensemble's conservative lines did little to hide my curves. Shrugging, I let it go. I wasn't about to starve myself to be fashionably thin. Instead, I hung up my jacket and reached for the top file stacked on my desk—a complex real estate fraud case with the deposition of our expert scheduled for Friday.

It only took ten minutes to accept that it was useless. My mind refused to focus. Sighing, I swiveled in my chair and logged onto my computer. "Angels, I need help," I said aloud, and sat back.

Everything started when we'd filed the dead lawyer case. Soon after, the CIA and Homeland Security conducted warrantless searches of our office, and then the US Attorney General tried to bribe us to dismiss the lawsuit. Yet with the case now over, what could *they*, whoever *they* were, possibly be involved in that they still felt the need to belatedly warn us to stop investigating? If we put Phil's revenge theory aside, the answer had to be that the murdered San Diego man was involved in something someone wanted us to stay away from.

I grabbed a pad from my desk and wrote: *1. SD man connected to something /someone shady* and looked at it. Okay next, the dead lawyer case really just exposed a way someone stole a lot of money. But if I looked at who'd responded to the lawsuit, I'd have to assume that someone was somehow connected to the government, in it or controlling it. Sadly, today's politicians and bureaucrats were puppets for contributions dispensed by large multinational conglomerates and kowtowed to their desires. I wrote: *2. Money stolen connected to government.* And of course, there was a hidden microchip with a picture of an unfamiliar coin: *3. Microchip, coin, and schematics.* I stared at the pad and found myself underlining the words *money, government,* and *coin.*

Well, they didn't say money was the root of all evil for nothing. Placing the pad aside, I typed *government conspiracies* in the search engine bar and following a hunch, added the word *currency*, and hit enter.

Two tenths of a second later—I had no idea why they told you that—I learned there were millions of cites. Scrolling down a few pages, I looked for clues to narrow my parameters. Finding none, I added the word *chronological* to get a timeline. A tenth of a second after I hit enter, my screen showed gazillions of entries. I moved the cursor down the pages, soon clicking on links and reading. After nearly an hour, I came to understand that the theories traced back to an advanced civilization named Atlantis, allegedly destroyed before recorded history. A surviving faction supposedly journeyed to Scotland and become the Druids, a pre-Christian Celtic society with practices steeped in mysticism. Claims that their progeny were scheming to rule the world abounded. Pretty crazy, I thought, looking at my notes.

Next were the Crusades Knights of Templar legends, which began circulating around the twelfth century. Apparently the Templars handed down ancient secrets found on the Temple Mount to a select few, and it was these men who started Freemasonry around the thirteenth century, even though Wikipedia said the fraternal organization of Freemasonry actually started in the sixteenth century. After that were the Illuminati. Although historically *Illuminati* referred to the Bavarian "enlightened" organization founded in 1776, it has come to mean a secret society manipulating world events. Conspiracy proponents assert Freemasonry is controlled by the shadowy Illuminati at the highest echelons, and they were the ones plotting global domination. These folks even claimed Jack the Ripper was a Freemason whose murders represented initiation rituals into the exalted Illuminati.

Yeesh, how did people come up with this stuff? Sighing, I sat back and closed my eyes. These claims were intriguing, and extremely entertaining, but not very helpful. Time to switch gears.

Sitting up, I deleted *chronological* and typed *latest* into the task bar and hit enter. Only ten thousand links this time. Okay, better. I started scrolling down the page. Articles about a number of secretive organizations were repeatedly captioned, and I wrote down their names. "The Round Table Plan" popped up several times, so I added it to my list. After moving down a few more pages, I stopped and clicked on "Dissecting the Round Table Plan."

Scholars who've studied the wealthy and powerful global elite believe the members of several private organizations have been working to consolidate political and economic power to create a global economic superpower. A one-world government named the New World Order— NWO—would be superior to the political governments of individual nations and rule the planet.

Well, someone always wants to rule the world, I thought and kept reading.

The Rockefeller, Carnegie, and Ford Foundations created by America's robber barons and bank industrialists planted the seeds of the NWO decades ago. Declaring their intent on every dollar since 1935, they marked our currency and took control of our monetary system, these elite who run the global economy through banks and manage the world's political puppets through think tanks they created, thus ensuring their continued hegemony over society.

A picture of a one-dollar bill followed. The Latin words on the back circled and translated—New World Order. You're kidding, I thought, and wrote them down. The author then accused the members of The Counsel on Foreign Relations, The Trilateral Commission, and The Bilderberg Group, of plotting a one-world government.

These three think tanks whose elite memberships run governments and multi-national conglomerates and include prominent media figures are fixing the fate of the world behind closed doors, encroaching on national sovereignty, and having the richest wield excessive influence over governments and news media. They are corrosive to a democratic society.

I pushed print and read a few more articles, before checking out the websites of the three organizations. I then clicked on a recent YouTube link. A Bilderberg Group founding member condescendingly told a reporter, "Accusations we're striving for a one-world government are exaggerated, but would a global community be bad?" The reporter responded by asking if he wanted a New World Order. Looking amused, he answered, "Possibly."

All right, you got me, I admitted, knowing I was hooked. By the number of links I found, these words had also sent conspiracy proponents into a frenzy, and reports of nefarious plots by allegedly sinister groups grew exponentially online.

I read and printed a few more articles, and sighed. Assuming folks were in fact plotting global domination, the real question became why. Why would anyone want to control the world? "Power, the aphrodisiac of the powerful," Oliver had once quoted. It might be the answer, but my gut told me there was a better reason. I just hadn't found it yet.

I sipped the last of my cold coffee, and sat back. Man, a lot of this was nuts. Okay, more than a lot. But even if part of it was true, how could someone control the world? Money, of course! Sitting up, I typed "how use money corruptly" in the search engine and pressed enter. I scanned the titles until I saw one labeled "Money for Dummies." Ask me a legal question, no problem, but finance... That I needed help with. So I clicked on the link and started reading. Apparently, a dollar is not just a dollar, but a sliding scale of value which changes based on how many dollars there are.

I printed the illustration explaining this, and looked at it. On the left was a box containing a pile of one hundred widgets and one hundred dollars. *What the heck is a widget?* They looked like circles to me, so I crossed out widgets and wrote cookies. Okay, one hundred cookies and one hundred dollars, equals one dollar each. On the right was a second box. One hundred cookies, and two hundred dollars, equal two dollars each. So by increasing the number of dollars, each cookie costs more and the dollar is worth less, and by decreasing the dollars, each cookie costs less and the dollar is worth more. Okay, that makes sense. But what really makes sense is if you knew when the amount of dollars was going to change, you could invest and make a lot of money. So who was the gatekeeper deciding when to add more dollars?

I then clicked on an article in *The Economist's Daily* titled "The Multinational Tragedy."

> Today's economic crisis was purposely created by the big multinational corporations. They forced a series of bailouts to flood the market with dollars, thereby reducing their value. Just look at which players made a fortune when this happened, and we'll know who caused our global financial meltdown.

Wow! So who made a mint? I also realized these folks weren't the gatekeeper, but the muscle manipulating the gatekeeper to add dollars. I pushed print.

Glancing at my watch, I saw that it was after four and logged off. The day had disappeared. The computer black hole into which time vanished happened once again. Sighing, I grabbed the huge jar of multicolored paper clips on my desk, and emptied it. When Ed walked into my office at five, he found me seated at my desk sorting. Pink, white, black, and red piles littered the surface.

"What're you doing?" he asked.

"Separating."

"I see. Any particular reason why?"

"I'm thinking. Separating is mindless and helps me think. Besides, I only use pink and white clips, but never black or red. They're bad luck."

"Excuse me?"

"Just accept it."

"Paper clips are lucky?"

"Ed, focus. Have you ever heard the phrase 'novus ordo seclorum'?"

"Novus what?"

"'Novus ordo seclorum,'" I repeated.

At his blank look, I pulled out my wallet and handed him a one-dollar bill. "Look on the back below the broken pyramid on the left." I waited for Ed's nod, and then continued. "It's been on the back of the United States one-dollar bill since 1935. It literally means 'New Order of the Ages,' but a lot of people say it really stands for 'New World Order' because the literal translation doesn't make any sense. The US didn't become an independent nation in 1935. It had already been one for more than 150 years."

"Fine, can we go now?" Ed asked, setting the dollar on my desk.

"In a minute. Now look at the Roman Numerals at the bottom of the pyramid."

Sighing, he picked up the dollar and read, "MDCCLXXVI."

"Or 1776, the year the Declaration of Independence was signed. It's also the year the Illuminati were supposedly founded."

"The Illuminati? Aren't there a lot of conspiracy theories about them?"

"Gazillions," I said, and asked Ed to read the stack of articles I'd printed.

"Can't you summarize it for me?"

"No. I need fresh eyes." Pausing, I said, "Please."

"That's a lot to read..."

"Fine, can I bribe you? What if I gave you an hour of slave time?"

"An hour? They're a lot of things I could ask you to do in that hour," Ed murmured.

"I know. Please."

"Okay," he said, and smiled. Funny how letting him think he could tell me what to do made him happy. We both knew he'd never ask me to do anything I wouldn't be comfortable with. It's that trust thing I acknowledged as I hugged him and said, "Thanks."

After dinner, Ed looked through the material while I pretended to watch a *Star Trek* video. By the time he finished reading, I was curled up on the sofa half asleep. "Well?"

"Most of it's crazy. Secret groups conspiring to take over the world, and multinationals intentionally creating the financial mess."

"Did you see the one about the BBC interview? Security for Bilderberg meetings are managed by military intelligence," I said.

"Yes, Rachel. I read everything."

"Well, their website says they're simply a lobby group. Lobby groups don't have military intelligence protect them."

Ed nodded. "You don't know if that's true, but I get your point. And I'm not saying I agree with the theories, just that they're possible. At least these wild accusations keep the media watching."

"Any other thoughts?" I asked.

"Well, I do believe there are people seeking to further their own agenda. But world domination? For what purpose? We're killing the planet, so why would they want it?"

"Good question. Maybe they know something we don't. Or maybe if they enslave the population, they could conserve the resources for the survival of a few."

"Anything's possible," Ed said with a shrug. "So are you going to tell me why you insisted I read this?"

"You know I see conspiracies everywhere," I said.

"True."

"So I wanted to know what you thought. Besides, we have a coin, and Phil mentioned a new coin, and… When can we speak with your economist guy? The sooner the better."

"Thursday. That's it? That's all you wanted?" Ed asked, looking at me suspiciously.

"At the moment."

"Okay. By the way, I'm cashing in my hour of slave time— now," Ed said.

"My pleasure."

. . .

I visited Oliver before going to work the next morning and brought the stack of articles I'd given Ed with me.

"What this?" he asked.

"Oh, a bunch of theories. I just want to know what you think."

Oliver nodded and then asked about the book in my hands. When I turned the cover toward him, he looked surprised.

"Plato wrote *The Republic* almost 2400 years ago, and talks about the immortality of the soul and his belief in reincarnation. He'd absolutely agree that we knew each other in a prior life."

"Then you'd both be crazy."

"Open mind, Oliver, open mind. I thought you might want to borrow it."

"Yes, well, I have something else you might enjoy." Oliver walked down the hall toward his study, and I followed. A large rolltop desk sat in the center of the square room, and every wall had floor-to-ceiling built-in shelves filled with books. Oliver reached for a book and winced.

"Oliver, are you okay?"

"Fine, fine, just a little stiff. Try this one, kiddo. My gift." He handed me a book titled *The Art of War* by Sun Tzu.

"What is it?"

"A military treatise written two hundred years before *The Republic* that's useful for litigation strategy. There are tips and advice on how to outsmart your opponent."

"Really? Thanks, Oliver," I murmured, flipping through the pages.

. . .

That evening I joined Oliver for a sunset swing. As soon as I walked into the living room, he pointed to the purple files sitting on the hall table.

"Purple?" I asked, and took a seat.

"For paranoid. I almost used red."

"Red?"

"For ridiculous."

"Come on Oliver, don't you buy any of it?"

"Did it ever occur to you or any of these conspiracy nuts, that world events might just be history unfolding and have nothing to do with conspiracies?"

"Nope. Oliver, there are books, and even documentaries on this stuff."

"Well, I think you all need to take a common sense pill and remember that government officials and big corporations perform illegal activities and routinely deceive the public. No mystery, no conspiracy, just what they do."

"But, how can you—"

"Rachel, the CIA has been involved in the illegal overthrow of foreign governments, and the FBI has spied on various groups in violation of Constitutional rights. Illegal actions, all authorized, by top government officials. There was no secret cabal orchestrating it to gain power, only our poor judgment in electing those in charge."

"Can't you remain open minded enough to allow that anything's possible?"

"Enough!"

"All right, all right." I held my hands up in surrender. "Let's just agree to disagree, okay?"

"Fine."

"Have you given any more thought to trying acupuncture? It'll help you sleep, Oliver."

"No. They use needles."

"Don't be a baby. They don't hurt."

"Easy for you to say."

"Oliver, acupuncture has been around for centuries. There are no adverse side effects unlike all those pills the doctor has you taking."

"No. I refuse to be a pin cushion."

"You are sooo stubborn."

"*I'm* stubborn? You're one to talk."

"Just think about it," I said.

"No." Oliver gave me a dirty look.

"Fine, I'm leaving. I can't talk to you when you're like this."

"I don't need to be afraid of bullets, just her," Oliver muttered as I walked away.

CHAPTER 10

The following evening I sat on one of the enormous blue damask sofas facing the wall of windows overlooking the bay in Phil's opulent home in Pacific Heights. Peter Simpson, the famous journalist, walked in, and I exclaimed, "Uncle Pete!" Jumping up, I ran over and hugged him. We'd met almost two years ago, and I'd adopted the curmudgeonly man as a favored uncle. Our relationship, founded on affection, involved pulling each other's chains. We both enjoyed the banter, and Phil told me Pete said it kept him on his toes.

"I am not your uncle!"

"Whatever you say, Uncle Pete."

He disentangled himself from my grasp, greeted Ed, and asked about Oliver's condition. Pete then took a seat on the sofa I'd vacated. I sat down next to him and stared adoringly, ignoring the hairy grey caterpillars above his eyes. Every night I watched him anchor the news and cringed at those eyebrows.

"We have something for you, Uncle Pete. Have you ever seen a magic key?" That grabbed his attention.

"Rachel, just tell me," Pete said with annoyance.

"Okay, Uncle Pete. And what I'm about to tell you is off the record."

"Fine, and for the last time, I am *not* your uncle."

"Yes, Uncle Pete." I told him about the key and the microchip. Phil handed him a copy of what Dr. Feden uncovered and we waited.

"Well, now I know why you asked me to look into that man, Phil. Does anyone know you have this?"

"We don't think so. Someone would have come after it. So what'd you find?" Phil asked.

"His name was John Bush—no relation," Pete said.

John Bush. I'd hated thinking of him as the murdered San Diego man, and was grateful to learn his identity. Pete also told us he was an ex-marine who'd become a mercenary after being discharged from the navy about ten years ago, and that he was highly skilled in combat, military hardware, and computers. It was rumored he did a number of jobs for Lockhead and Hillman, the two largest defense companies, here and overseas.

"What I still don't understand is why he was willing to talk to you folks," Pete said.

"No idea, and since he's dead we'll never know," Ed said.

"Well, I'd like to think he was trying to do the right thing," I told them.

"Naïve," Phil said, and I scowled at him.

"I agree. Any idea how he got the chip?" Pete asked, and Ed told him no.

"There was a story I did back in '08 about an Aussie woman and an MP3 player." At our blank looks Pete told us about an Australian woman who'd bought a used MP3 player at an Oklahoma thrift store while on vacation. When she connected the device to her computer she found data on Iraq military missions, and a journalist later confirmed that the information was correct. "Basically, it's not uncommon for military information to end up stolen, and there's a growing black market for it," Pete said.

"So because he worked for defense companies, and they're connected to the military, he may have gotten into their systems and found the data on the microchip?" I asked. That sounded really far-fetched to me.

"Possibly. Remember the story I did on the Pentagon hack

three years ago?" Pete asked, and I watched Ed and Phil shake their heads. "Do you folks ever watch my newscasts?"

"I do, Uncle Pete, always." I then recounted the show where the Chinese People's Liberation Army got into the Pentagon and Defense Department computers. They had to shut down parts of their network because classified information was breached.

"Yes, Rachel, thank you. And what I'm getting at is a person with access and the right know-how could find a lot of things someone might want hidden," Pete said, and sat back. He sighed deeply. "There've been rumors of a new currency for years, but this... What do you need from me?"

Phil told him to hold off on the microchip, and we'd give him an exclusive. He then explained that we also needed him for leverage and showed him a copy of the threatening note he received two weeks ago. We'd reported it to the police, but they had no leads. If Pete could do a story on it, then whoever shot Oliver and sent the note would know that we'd give everything we had to the media, and hopefully they'd back off.

"Are you okay, Phil?" Pete asked.

"I'm scared, but we're safest figuring out what's going on," Phil said, tugging at his bow tie.

"Okay, what else can I do?" Pete asked, and Ed told him his piece should also include how Oliver was still in a coma, and devastated and afraid, Phil had decided to retire.

"I am *not* retiring!"

"Phil, Ed just said you want me to tell everyone you are," Pete said.

"I'm only pretending to retire." Phil's arms were rigidly crossed in front of him.

"Just agree," I said with exasperation.

Pete looked at Phil, and then at me. "Okay, you're retiring, but you're not really retiring."

"Just so we're all clear," Phil added.

"And you tell me I'm nuts," I muttered, and Phil gave me a dirty look.

"Yes, well, I think I'll get going. I have a feeling a family squabble is about to begin, and I plan to be long gone."

"Sorry, Uncle Pete. Some of us have issues."

CHAPTER 11

"Hi, I'm Rachel," I said, walking into Oliver's den Thursday evening.

"K. Bixler," the woman responded, and nodded crisply. She was lovely with her willowy Nordic looks, and tailored yellow suit. Smiling I asked, "Is the *K* for Katherine?"

"No. The letter *K*."

"Just the letter *K*? It's not short for anything?"

"No," she said.

Strange. I sat next to Ed. When Phil and William showed up a few moments later, Ed introduced K, and said he'd asked her here to give us a crash course in economics. He then invited our questions so she could tailor the discussion.

I looked at K and realized she was quite pretty in an intellectual sort of way. John might be interested, and we could still use the good karma.

"Are you single?"

"Excuse me?" K, just the letter K, seemed confused.

"Ignore her," Phil said, and asked why a government would make new coins.

"Do you mean add a new coin or replace the existing currency like they did with the euro?"

"Let's go with replace, but in America," Phil said, and K's left eyebrow rose. "Just a line of inquiry," Phil added, and Ed motioned for her to start.

"Okay, I'm going to go over a number of basics first, beginning with the Federal Reserve," K said, and explained that it was a banking system created in 1913, that was *supposedly* designed to preserve economic stability and prevent banking problems. The Fed loaned money to banks, and decided when to distribute new currency.

"They're the gatekeeper!"

"Is there a problem?" K asked.

"No, please continue," Phil said, and scowled at me.

Shrugging, K defined inflation, and a recession. When she started on something called stagflation I tuned her out, instead thinking about the cookie illustration and how increasing or decreasing the number of dollars allows you to fiddle with its value.

"But how can all our dollars be backed by gold?" Phil asked, interrupting my thoughts.

"They're not," K said. "FDR took the United States off the gold standard and required Americans to turn in their gold coins in exchange for dollars."

"So our money's not worth anything?"

"Rachel, US dollars are backed by the confidence people have in our country," K said.

She had to be kidding.

Phil's cell phone rang, and he glanced down. "Sorry, I need to answer this. Can we take a break?"

K nodded, so I stood and walked down the hall to Oliver's study, where he was watching and listening in on the security camera monitor sitting on his desk. "Hey there," I greeted.

"She's making my head hurt."

"Maybe this will help." I handed Oliver a cookie, and his face lit up.

"I have two questions. What did K mean when she said the Fed was *supposedly* designed to keep the economy stable? And what happened to all that gold we turned in?" Oliver then held out his hand.

"What?"

"Where's the rest of the cookies?"

"Only one. You're a cookieholic."

"So?" he said with a grin.

When I returned to the den, I found everyone waiting for me. Sitting, I asked Oliver's questions.

"You're right, I did say *supposedly*. There are a number of rogue economists, myself included, who wonder whether the Federal Reserve is merely a cover for certain wealthy people."

"It's a conspiracy. I just knew it." I moved forward on my seat.

"Shush, Rachel." Phil nodded at K.

"Let's start with money. It's a convenient medium of exchange. But this tool can also be used corruptly by playing with its value."

Now she was talking my game, and I asked how.

"History shows us." K explained that easy credit marked the 1920s. Fueled by investor overconfidence and speculation, many purchased stock on credit in anticipation of future stock price increases. This in turn formed a market bubble of inflated prices compared to true stock earnings, creating a bloated stock market resting on a wobbly foundation of credit. The Federal Reserve knocked over the unsteady legs beneath the market by severely contracting credit. The predictable result was the inability of investors to cover their margin or credit purchases, forcing them to sell stock at fire-sale prices to raise cash. And unpaid loans also meant our nation's banks had no cash flow and couldn't function. Meanwhile, having set everything in motion, the Fed just stood back and watched the frenzy escalate and the stock market crash, and ignored pleas for help as banks collapsed.

"But you said the Federal Reserve is supposed to preserve banking stability." William frowned and unwrapped a peppermint candy.

"Again, supposedly."

"I don't know. You're attributing malice to what could possibly be explained by the Fed's stupidity," Phil said.

"Even though it's happening all over again?" K told us that during the recent housing boom, it was easy to obtain a mortgage leading a lot of people to invest and speculate. Houses appraised at artificially inflated prices, and banks and corporations held the paper on these loans. When the bubble burst, housing prices plummeted, and those stuck with these paper loan assets lost billions since the homes securing them were only worth a fraction of the loan amount.

Further, homeowners also had no equity in their homes because they lost their value. And with no equity, they stopped paying their mortgages, and banks lost a significant portion of their liquid capital. Mortgage payments were the cash flow banks depended on to function, and without it, credit lines quickly closed, and the banking world started to grind to a halt.

"So, enter the stimulus packages delivering billions to prevent a massive depression like in the thirties," Phil said, and K agreed.

"If people were orchestrating the situation, say over-appraising homes for mortgages, their prior knowledge would allow them to avoid significant financial losses?" I asked.

"Absolutely. They'd sell off their assets at the inflated value, and wait," K said.

"And when the economy tanked, they'd be in a position to buy up real estate and businesses for a song," Phil said.

"And once the economy revived, assets would regain their value, and they would make a fortune," K said.

"K, I'm curious. With all the bailout money flooding the market, our currency's lost a lot of value. Could the government recall our dollars and exchange them for a new currency?" Phil asked.

"It's possible," K said, and Phil and I looked at each other.

"Wow, this is a lot to absorb." I smiled at K.

Phil suggested we stop and continue at a later date, and everyone agreed. Ed thanked K, and Phil and William stood to shake her hand.

I waited until K was putting on her coat to corner her. "That was very helpful. I was wondering, if our dollars were recalled and exchanged for a new currency, its value could also be manipulated, couldn't it?"

She said, "Yes."

CHAPTER 12

Once K left, Oliver joined us in the den. Phil was already pacing, and William was pouring a scotch. Oliver made a beeline for the open liquor cabinet, and pulled out a tin of cookies. "Energy food," he said, and removed two.

I sat down on the sofa next to Ed and closed my eyes, exhausted. When I felt him take my hand and lace his fingers through mine, I relaxed, and let my head fall back. I was on overload. Even so, I could feel the energy pinging off Phil. Sighing, I opened my eyes and sat up. "Okay Phil, what?"

"Who raked it in when the economy tanked?"

"Uncle Pete would know."

"Right." Still pacing, Phil pulled his phone from his pants pocket. "Hi, it's Phil. Who cashed in the most when the real estate market went belly up?" A moment later he hung up. "He'll get back to me in the morning."

I looked at Oliver. Slumped in a recliner, his face a bit flushed, he seemed worn out.

"Oliver, you okay?" I went over and felt his forehead. No fever.

"I'm a bit tired, that's all."

Phil stopped pacing and stared at Oliver. "That's all?"

"Yes, Phil, that's all. Stop fussing." Oliver wiped cookie crumbs from his lap.

"Fine. It's late and I'm going home." Phil grabbed his coat.

Abrupt, but understood. Oliver's health took priority.

• • •

The next day I found myself locked in the conference room, defending the deposition of our forensic accountant, an expert witness in the real estate fraud case I was handling. Eager to know what Phil learned, I texted him during a morning break. He later texted back "see O." As soon as I got home, I changed out of my suit and went upstairs. Wayne greeted me from his post near the elevator, and told me Oliver was in the den.

"Hey Oliver, how ya feeling?" I asked walking in.

"Fine, just like I was when you checked three hours ago."

"Good. What are you watching?"

"A documentary on the round stone tower in Rhode Island. They'll break for pledges in a minute, and we'll talk."

I took a seat and picked up today's newspaper from the coffee table. A story about the threatening note and Phil's retirement was circled on page three. When they interrupted the program to ask for donations, Oliver said, "It's called the Newport Tower. It's made of stone, has eight sides, and was also called a baptistery. You went there to cleanse away your sins and be born again."

"Eight sides?"

"Eight's the number of infinity, and if cleansed, you'll live forever. What's interesting is the Templars used the octagon inside a circle design before 1400."

"The Knights of Templar?" I asked.

"Yes. This tower is the only one like it in the United States."

"The Templars were in America before 1400? Before Christopher Columbus?"

"I know it's controversial. But remember, history is the lie commonly agreed upon." Oliver switched off the TV.

"So what'd you guys find out?" I asked.

"Phil spoke with Pete this morning, and then he came by here."

"And?"

"The biggest winners were the folks who worked at Nationview Bank. They made a fortune."

"I thought they went out of business." Their logo, a red imprint of our country with their name in black capital letters written across it, was once advertised everywhere.

"They did. There's a file by the door."

I turned and saw a thick yellow folder. "Yellow?"

"Canary...for con men. Go home, we'll talk tomorrow."

Downstairs, I made a fresh pot of coffee, and opened the file on the kitchen table. A bulky overnight envelope addressed to Phil from Pete's news station sat on top. I pulled out its contents and delved in.

Nationview Bank, a leading financial institution, had funded a staggering amount of sub-prime home loans even though most borrowers couldn't afford the loan payments once the adjustable interest rate reset to the higher prime rate. The loans were marketed on the theory that real estate prices would keep going up. Borrowers could then pull out the increased equity to pay the mortgage when the loan amount increased. The lender never warned that assuming home prices would continue rising was in fact a gamble, and not guaranteed.

Nationview's top executives then "coincidently" left their positions and sold millions in stock options a year before the company went under investigation and collapsed. Pooling their ill-gotten riches, they funded a new start-up called Liberty Mortgage Admittance Company, which they pitched as "Liberty Mac." It sounded like another Washington bailout operation to me. Liberty Mac made money by buying loans from struggling or failed financial institutions at huge discounts. So even if it slashed interest rates, or made other loan modifications to entice borrowers into resuming payments, the company would still profit tremendously.

"Fascinating," I murmured, refilling my cup. These folks created the home loan mess, made a fortune off it, and are cashing in again.

The next materials were about Gordon Lincoln Dillingham. As the former president of Nationview, and the new face of

Liberty Mac, he and his team of cronies had been busy buying up delinquent home mortgages the government took over from other failed banks. I found a copy of yesterday's *Financial Times* near the bottom and turned to the tabbed page.

A highlighted article captioned "Nationview's Unscrupulous Execs Make Fortune off Havoc Created" grabbed my attention. They'd just closed an impressive deal with the Federal Deposit Insurance Corporation (FDIC) paying 51.6 million dollars for 730 million dollars worth of mostly delinquent residential loans left from First National Bank of Atlanta's failure last year. Liberty Mac's payment was the equivalent of fourteen cents on the dollar, and their agreement with the FDIC allowed them to keep twenty cents of every dollar it collected. So even if they slashed the delinquent loan amounts in half, with interest they still stood to make more than eleven billion dollars.

"Eleven billion dollars," I said in awe. These folks were brilliant—and evil.

"Babe, I'm home," I heard Ed call out.

I put the paper down and went to greet him, eager to share the news.

• • •

The following morning I reached across the bed for Ed's warm body and touched a note on his cold pillow: "I know it's Saturday. I need to go into the office for a few hours. Stay put! Love you, Me."

Getting out of bed, I padded across the room to push the thick white curtain aside and look out the window. It was a beautiful sunny day. A quick walk over to the pier to visit the sea lions was what I desperately needed. Over a month after the shooting, and in broad daylight, it should be fine. That decided, I made a cup of coffee, got dressed, and left. Being outside and moving felt wonderful. I walked over to the pier, saw the sea lions, and took the circuitous route home. West along the wharf to

Ghiradelli Square before turning uphill at Polk. I had just crossed Union when I felt an uncomfortable feeling between my shoulder blades, a heavy pressure of someone watching me and my body's discomfort warning me to beware.

Alarmed, I turned toward a restaurant window and pretended to read the menu while peering about. Yuppies with coffee cups and strollers passed by. A man in jogging attire walking his dog. Nothing stuck out as suspicious, so I continued down Polk Street on alert. Ed was going to kill me if whoever was following me didn't get me first. Pulling out my cell phone, I ducked into the beauty supply store near the corner of Green.

"May I help you?" The blond woman behind the counter smiled.

"No thanks. Just looking." I punched in Ed's number on speed dial. Blast, it rolled over into voicemail. I disconnected the call and pretended interest in the hair products while watching the front window. I then moved behind a tall display and picked up a pink shampoo bottle, faking absorption. I still didn't see anything unusual outside. A moment later I left to the tinkle of bells jingling above the door. I'd gone about three steps when the heavy feeling between my shoulder blades returned. *Crap, crap, crap*, I soundlessly screamed, before ducking into the newsstand on the next block. I joined the queue and called Ed again. His voicemail picked up, and I told him to phone. I then tried John. When the call rolled into his voicemail, I hung up.

Okay, I was really scared. My heart hammered and that heavy feeling got more intense. Whoever followed me was nearby. What was I going to do? I tried not to panic. I nearly jumped when I felt someone tap me on my right shoulder. Turning, I looked into the same unusual green-color eyes as mine. But the woman was about ten years older.

"Are you okay?"

"What?"

"Can I help?"

"I'm sorry, have we met?" She seemed familiar.

"No, I don't think so. But I heard you," she said, staring at me.

"Heard me? I didn't say any..." My thoughts? I stared back at her. She nodded.

"Miss, you want anything?" the clerk interrupted.

I hadn't realized I was at the front of the newsstand's line.

"Oh, ah, lottery ticket." I gave him a dollar. He handed me the slip of paper, and I moved over to the magazine rack.

Seconds later the green-eyed lady followed. "He's across the street by the hardware store."

I didn't ask how she knew. I just knew she did.

"Walgreens is two blocks up on the corner. The pharmacy's in the back, and there's a rear exit to the street."

Her voice also sounded familiar, but before I could try to figure out why, she said, "Be careful. Now go."

I nodded and did as she directed, my heart racing as I walked the two blocks without looking behind me. It was the longest two blocks I'd ever walked, and I felt like everyone was staring at me. The pressure between my shoulders was excruciating. A few minutes later I convinced a female clerk to let me out the back by claiming an old boyfriend was following me. I was scared, and it showed. Once outside, I moved east on Broadway before heading uphill and making my way home. My phone rang just as I unlocked the front door.

"What's up?" Ed asked.

"Oh, nothing." I closed the door behind me and turned the deadbolt. I then leaned against the door and sank to the floor, letting the tears flow.

"Rachel?" I heard Ed say.

"Sorry, bad reception."

"You sound kind of funny."

"Really? I was about to take a bath."

"Are you sure you're okay?"

"Positive," I said, now that I was safe, and quickly ended the call. He was too perceptive.

Soaking among the fragrant bubbles, I tried to relax, but my mind wouldn't stop thinking about what just happened. I wanted to tell Ed. I wanted to tell Oliver. But they'd only yell at me, and I already knew I'd been foolish. Why bother.

So, who was following me?

And better yet, who was that woman?

• • •

Drained, I slipped into bed for a quick nap after my bath. Sounds in the kitchen woke me. I threw on sweats and walked down the hall to find a note on the kitchen table. *Upstairs at O's, love ya, E* I read just as the intercom buzzed. Startled, I jumped, dropping the message. Calm down! I looked at the security monitor. It was only John.

"Hi there," I greeted moments later. I noticed the outline of a gun holster under his brown sweatshirt and shivered.

"You, okay?" John asked, and I nodded. He then told me Ed asked him to stop by.

"He's at Oliver's." I went with him upstairs.

Ed and Oliver were laughing when we walked into Oliver's den. "What's so funny?" I asked. They stopped laughing and exchanged a look.

John cleared his throat and took a seat. I waited. The silence grew uncomfortable.

"Well, if you must know… It's you," Oliver said.

"Me? I'm funny?"

"Kiddo, you do realize that you're peculiar, don't you?" Oliver asked.

"Oliver, did you just call me peculiar?"

"Only in the best way," he said, and I stared at him.

"Okay, I'm funny, possibly peculiar. So, what were you two laughing about?"

"I told Oliver about your color thing, and he already knew," Ed said.

"Bad people and danger have red and black around them, pink, white and gold are for good," I explained.

"I did say peculiar," Oliver said.

"Okay, I'm peculiar… Whatever." I'd had enough of this conversation, and told Oliver that I'd Googled the Newport Tower and learned there were a number of people who believed a Scottish mason, Prince Henry Sinclair, befriended the Templars and helped them sail to America in the 1300s.

Henry Sinclair? That's my name.

I turned and stared at John. "Henry Sinclair's your real name, John?" I never believed his true name was John Smith.

"I didn't say that."

"You just did."

"Not out loud," John said, raising his brows in disbelief. Ed and Oliver started laughing.

"She does it to you too?" Oliver asked, and Ed nodded, still laughing. John looked confused.

"Sometimes she hears what you're thinking. It's random. I've pretty much gotten used to it," Ed explained, smiling.

"She can hear people's thoughts?" John's eyes widened.

"I did say she's peculiar," Oliver pointed out.

"*She* is getting mad, fellas. Are you done?" I asked, crossing my arms in front of me.

"Yes, dear," Ed said, and Oliver laughed again. Once his mirth died down, Oliver told me he'd called Ed and requested a background check on Dillingham. I was about to ask how long it would take when Ed said, "Tomorrow."

Seems that I wasn't the only one who read minds.

CHAPTER 13

When I woke the next morning, I found a note on Ed's pillow again: "Be home in a few hours, love ya, E." The Sunday paper and a freshly brewed pot of coffee were waiting for me when I walked into the kitchen. I poured a mug and sat to divide the newspaper into two stacks, one pile to read and the other to discard. Once separated, I'd organize the read stack in the order I liked to peruse it. The last section always contained the weather. It was my favorite part, and I saved if for the end, like dessert.

Although I haven't actually traveled to many places, I planned to, and knowing a city's weather will be useful. How was Paris in July? Or Dubai in December? I realized it was a bit weird, but one day I will go to these places and at the right time—the right weather time.

So I sipped my coffee, and read about national and world news, followed by upcoming sales. I scanned reviews of the new movies, and saw the latest fashion trends. Next were the society pages. Phil's wife, Lynn, attended most of the reported events, so I'd switched the society pages to the read pile, and found I enjoyed them. Apparently, Friday's fundraiser for the opera had been a grand success according to those quoted. I then looked at the photos and choked. Coffee sloshed over the side of the mug, and I set it down. Drawing a deep breath, I looked again. A grinning photo of Gordon Lincoln Dillingham stared back at me. I read

the accompanying blurb about a fundraiser Dillingham's father
was hosting next week and moved the paper aside. Picking up the
mug, I took another sip. And then another.

Random thoughts raced through my mind, and I felt the urge to
go outside and walk the labyrinth. But I couldn't, not after yesterday.
I was too afraid. I took another sip and picked up the sports section.
The weather was on its back page. It was 108 in Red Bluff and 96
in Montreal. Paris and Madrid approached 80, and were cloudy.
Sighing, I gathered all the papers to toss in the recycle bin, and
refilled my cup. What to do? What to do? And then I knew. If
Muhammad can't come to the mountain, you improvise. My condo,
shaped like a square with a hallway down the center, was perfect.

After changing into sweats, I walked into the living room
and pushed the sofa, chair, and coffee table against the left wall.
For once I was grateful Ed had insisted on hanging the enormous
TV. There was now an empty space in the center of the room.
Grabbing a roll of toilet paper from the bathroom and some tape
from my office, I knelt at the front door and taped the end to the
floor. I then stood and gave the toilet paper a gentle shove and
watched it roll all the way down the hall to my bedroom door. I
secured it near the bed and rolled it into the adjacent living room
and around the center perimeter, and back down the hall toward
the front door, taping as needed. After repeating this several times
my maze was done.

Standing at the front door, I took a number of deep breaths,
and started walking alongside the white path. Mounds of gold
coins, and the Nationview crimson logo appeared in my mind.
Fleeting images of Oliver and the gold key with Dillingham's
society photo swirling around it followed. Blazing fires burning US
dollars in the hulls of canoes on a lake, and the glassy unblinking
eyes of John Bush materialized next. And then all went black.

I stood still in the living room trying to decipher the insights.
Gold, dollars, and death surfaced. How it all fit, I didn't know. For
now, I replaced the phrase "Cash is King" with "Gold is Golden,"
and Mr. Gordon Lincoln Dillingham—even his initials almost

spelled gold—was somehow connected to Oliver's shooting. Of this I felt certain.

When Ed said, "What?" I looked up and saw him staring at the toilet paper all over the floor. I hadn't heard him come home.

"What?" he repeated, waving his hand about.

Walking over, I hugged him. I had the real deal.

Dillingham was just the fool's version.

• • •

Once I'd explained the toilet paper, Ed handed me the dossier on Dillingham. He'd already given Oliver a copy. "Almost nothing before he started running Nationview thirty years ago," Ed told me.

"That's bizarre." I opened the file. It disclosed Dillingham's date of birth, August 8, 1950, in Slovenia; driver's license and social security numbers; date of marriage to Stella Winthrop, January 1, 1985; that he had no children; and details of his vast assets, bank accounts, stock, and real estate holdings. It also provided information on the Gordon and Stella Dillingham Foundation, started three years ago, containing four million dollars in assets. A second charity named after Gordon's father, The Charles Dillingham Foundation, held twenty million. The senior Dillingham was in his eighties and emigrated from Slovenia to America in the late sixties. By 1975, he was the president of an Arizona savings and loan bank that failed in the mid-1980s.

A chill passed through me, and I shivered. The file fell to the floor. Shadows enveloped me, and that familiar heaviness pressed into my back. And then the darkness and weight lifted as suddenly as it came, leaving my heart hammering and my body shaken. *What was that?*

"Rachel, what's wrong? You're trembling."

"I don't know." I reached down and picked up the file, and stared at it. The feeling didn't return. Sighing, I set it down on the coffee table and took Ed's extended hand.

When I joined Oliver for a sunset swing later that afternoon, he asked what I thought about Dillingham.

"Which one?" I said.

"Remember when the S&Ls were deregulated in the '80s?"

"Oliver, I was five."

"The banks made risky investments with their depositors' money. Hundreds failed, and the FDIC had to pay billions. Well, really the US taxpayer," Oliver said.

"So this isn't the first time we've bailed out the financial people."

"Privatize profits and socialize losses is the banking way."

"And the Dillinghams learned that decades ago," I said.

"Everything about them is suspicious."

"It at least makes you wonder."

Oliver nodded and kept swinging. Beyond the window, the stars were out in full force, twinkling in the inky night sky, and it was beautiful. When Oliver said he was getting tired, I wished him good night and headed home to find Ed cooking dinner.

I just love a man wearing an apron—and nothing else.

• • •

After supper Ed and I watched a video and went to bed early. The next thing I knew I was screaming. It took a moment for me to realize where I was and stop.

"Rachel, honey, what is it?" Ed asked. "You're white as a sheet."

I looked at him, and my eyes welled.

"What's wrong? You're scaring me," Ed said, reaching for me. "You're drenched."

Chilled, I started shivering.

"No, I can't tell you," I said, shaking my head and moving closer. "No, no, no," I repeated into his neck as the tears flowed and images assaulted me. I felt like I couldn't breathe, and started gasping for air.

"Rachel, look at me," Ed directed, setting me a foot away. "Take a deep breath."

I heard the worry in his voice, and knew I was incoherent, but I couldn't help it. I clenched my eyes shut, and tried to breathe as I watched Ed get shot. Blood was everywhere, and I couldn't reach him no matter how hard I tried. And then I remembered lying on a dirt floor, my hands bound with rope, unable to move. A man said Ed was dead, and I'd screamed to make it untrue.

"Honey, it was just a dream."

"No, no, no, it was real," I sobbed, as the hazy image of a man with black soulless eyes stared at me.

Ed continued to hold me until I quieted. He then removed my wet T-shirt and slipped one of his over my head, before wrapping himself around me. "You're safe," he whispered in my ear. "Go to sleep."

Hours later I watched the sky lighten as I lay awake, my hand on Ed's chest, feeling the steady beat of his heart.

CHAPTER 14

Monday dawned sunny and warm, the city caressed by soft bay breezes. It was also a holiday, and over morning coffee I'd convinced Ed we should take an urban hike through North Beach and continue up to the top of Telegraph Hill to Coit Tower, the 210-foot art deco building made of unpainted reinforced concrete. Built in 1933, and according to urban legend, the builders designed the structure to resemble a fire-hose nozzle in tribute to the 1906 earthquake firefighters. Today it stood as an icon of the San Francisco skyline, with panoramic views, and walls displaying incredible hand-painted murals.

On the way back we crossed Columbus Avenue and continued south to Vallejo Street. I felt the warmth of my angels embrace as we neared the Mona Lisa restaurant and slowed. Drawing closer, I peered in the window. Holding court at the center of the bar stood a tall, bespectacled Italian man in his forties, whom I'd fondly dubbed the Mayor of Columbus Ave., the main street traversing North Beach, the Italian section of town. Stefano had his hand on the pulse of the city at all times, and most days you'd find him walking through the heart of various neighborhoods, glad-handing all the shopkeepers. Except Mondays. Mondays he relaxed at the Mona Lisa.

Of course! Stefano knew everybody. He could get us into Dillingham's party.

"Thank you, angels," I whispered.

And then I caught a man's reflection behind us and jerked around. No one was there, just the normal afternoon passersby. Man, I was jumpy. But then that heavy pressure between my shoulders returned, and I felt even more uneasy. "Let's go in," I said, grabbing Ed's hand. Delicious aromas and numerous Mona Lisa pictures greeted us when we walked inside.

"Rachel, Ed, how are you? And how's Oliver?" Stefano inquired as we made our way over. Once the bartender took our drink orders, Ed told him that Oliver was still in a coma.

"It's been difficult," I said trying to appear upset. When our drinks arrived, I took a fortifying sip. "Stefano, my dear friend, who knows everyone."

That caused him to smile. "So, how can I help you?"

"Are you a mind reader?"

His smile grew into a grin, and he waited for me to continue. "Do you know the Dillinghams?"

"Dillingham," he repeated, pushing his eyeglasses higher with his index finger.

"They're involved in a fundraiser for something or other in Marin on Saturday. It was mentioned in yesterday's *Chronicle*."

"Okay." He nodded. "And?"

"Well, I was hoping we could somehow get invited."

Stefano stared at me a second. "You're up to something." This time I grinned and waited for him to continue. "Call me tomorrow," he said and wrote his cell number on a slip of paper.

I smiled my thanks as Ed nudged me and angled his chin toward the painting on the back wall. "Did you see that?"

"Yes, Ed."

"Isn't the Mona Lisa supposed to have clothes on?"

"Art is in the eye of the beholder."

• • •

As soon as we left the restaurant Ed asked me what was going on.

"We need to meet Dillingham, and the party is a perfect way."

"Why?"

"Because he's somehow connected to Oliver's shooting," I said, as we turned west on Union Street toward home.

"There's no proof of that."

"Ed, I feel it." I took his hand and we continued walking uphill, our labored breathing filling the silence.

"Your instincts work better than my equipment sometimes," he finally said, smiling wryly. "I haven't made any headway on the woods or factory, and the coin itself doesn't incriminate anyone… Okay, fine."

Winded, I just squeezed Ed's hand and kept walking.

• • •

I phoned Stefano the following afternoon. "You're all set," he said, and gave me the details. I then called Lynn. Phil's wife was an expert in couture or costume design as I thought of it, and my discount shopping wouldn't suffice. Since I needed to wear the appropriate clothes to the fundraiser, it was better to ask for help and let the professional handle it.

Two days later, Lynn showed up at my front door with her bodyguard, Ken. Phil was not taking any chances with her safety. I bent and hugged Lynn's tiny form, feeling her wispy blond hair brush my cheek, and stepped back. Dressed in a cream Chanel suit, with diamonds twinkling in her ears, she was over sixty and still beautiful, and the epitome of class and elegance.

Ken on the other hand was serious blond eye candy, and holding numerous shopping bags. He said, "Hello," and I suggested he might want to wait in the kitchen where I had placed freshly baked cookies and coffee. Ken smiled. He handed me the packages, and Lynn walked with me toward the bedroom. On the way she asked what I was up to.

"I'm not sure yet. Just following a hunch."

I set the bags on the bed and started unpacking. Three dresses, a low-cut form-fitting gold lamé gown, an empire-waist emerald silk long dress, and a classic knee-length beaded black cocktail number, emerged.

When I eyed the remaining bags, Lynn said, "I picked up a few other outfits."

Sighing, I didn't argue, instead dutifully tried everything on. Once we'd finished, Lynn pulled out a sheaf of folded receipts from her Birkin bag and handed them to me. I nearly choked.

"You told me to purchase what you'd need. It's an investment," she said.

"It's groceries for a family for a year."

"If you plan on moving in certain circles, you will need to dress accordingly."

Fully aware that no one ever won an argument with Lynn, not even Phil, I said, "Yes, ma'am," and thanked her profusely. I gave her a check, and then showed her and Ken out. Ed came home twenty minutes later.

"So, how do you feel about ramen noodles?" I wrapped my arms around him.

"What?" he mumbled into my hair.

"Well, it's what we'll be eating for awhile. I asked Lynn for help purchasing an outfit for Dillingham's party, and now we're the proud owners of a small fortune in clothes. That is unless *you* want to tell Lynn to return them?"

"No way. Ramen noodles are my favorite."

"I thought you'd say that."

•   •   •

Ed picked me up after work on Friday, and we drove back to my condo. He needed to return a few phone calls, so I waited for him in the living room, gathering my thoughts and staring at the gold key in my hands. The duplicate gold key that is. The original key and microchip were still with Dr. Feden.

Ed was not going to like what I was about to suggest. But as Master Sun Tzu taught, secret operations are essential in war. And this was war. This key literally was the key. I needed to wear it. When Ed came into the living room and took a seat on the sofa, I stood, and then sat on his lap and draped myself around him.

"What do you want?"

"Just you." I nuzzled his neck.

"This feels wonderful, but are you going to tell me what you want?"

I snuggled a bit closer before explaining my idea to wear the key to tomorrow's event. Ed stiffened, and then stood with me in one fluid motion. He set me down a foot away from him, and looked me in the eyes. "Not happening, Rachel."

"But if they're involved, this may tell us."

"No! I agreed to go, nothing more." He crossed his arms in front of him and wore a mulish expression. This was going to require finesse.

"Okay, let's talk reasonably." I took a seat on the sofa. When I motioned for him to sit next to me, he sat on the nearby chair. Not good. "Ed, I'm simply wearing a house key on a chain. If no one cares, then it's a dead end. But if I'm right, and there is a reaction…" I ended with a shrug.

"Too dangerous." He shook his head.

"We're like sitting ducks right now, and this key is our only lead."

"No!"

"I'm going to do it anyway, so you may as well agree."

"Rachel." His tone was a warning.

"Ed, I'm tired of being scared and worrying about everyone." Taking a chance, I told him what happened on my walk to the pier.

"What?" he yelled turning red. "How could you have been so stupid?"

I cringed. I'd never seen him this angry. Okay, maybe I deserved it, but I needed to stay focused. I took a deep breath and relaxed my shoulders. "Ed, I can't be afraid all the time. Please." I touched his arm, but he shrugged my hand away. A vein throbbed in his neck.

Tears beckoned, and I looked away. He had to understand this was the only way. So I waited, growing more and more uncomfortable with each passing moment.

"If you say someone was following you, someone was," he finally said.

"And if nothing happens, then that'll be the end of it."

"Let me think about it," Ed said, reaching for the *Star Wars* video I'd placed on the coffee table.

• • •

Ed waited in the living room while I got ready for the party the following evening. When I joined him dressed in my new gold dress, his appreciative smile turned into a grimace. "I hate this," he said, eyeing my décolletage.

"I know, but you agreed. Dillingham could be connected to Oliver's shooting. And don't worry," I said, placing my hand on his arm. "I have my own personal über hot bodyguard to protect me." When he didn't even crack a grin, I added, "Besides, the latest fashion trend is to wear key pendants—Tiffany's started it."

"Fine, whatever. Let's go."

"Yes, dear." Leaning over, I kissed his cheek. I then picked up my purse and slipped my arm through his.

We were driving north over the Golden Gate Bridge when Ed told me he'd attached a small video camera to his lapel.

"Why do we need that?"

"You never know when scoping out possible enemy territory will come in handy. Especially if you're right, and they have something to do with shooting Oliver," Ed said.

Goose bumps rose on my arms, and I felt chilled.

It only took twenty minutes to get to the senior Dillingham's Mill Valley residence. A uniformed attendant stopped us at the front gate and checked to see that our name was on the list. He waved us through and toward the valet.

Moments later we walked inside the brightly lit house crowded with couture-swathed elite. Diamonds and jewels glittered everywhere. I passed an A-list movie star wearing an intricately beaded long red dress talking to a Grammy-award-winning singer swathed in a crystal-encrusted floor-length white gown. Thank goodness Lynn had dressed me, I thought as we moved through the lavishly adorned crowds. Crystal chandeliers hung from the vaulted ceilings highlighting the myriad of gilded antiques amid large black-and-gold brocade furnishings. When my eyes locked with a man speaking into a head mic, the goose bumps returned. Grabbing Ed's hand, I followed his circuitous pattern through the house as he filmed. I could now see that tables of food and liquor filled the back patio and an eating area off to the right. A small band softly played music to the left. Center stage, however, drew my attention. There, the Dillinghams held court with Old D bracketed by his son and wife. Four large muscular men stood nearby.

I felt Old D staring at my chest the moment we joined the receiving line. His gaze focused below my neck, and I knew it wasn't my rack getting his attention. We introduced ourselves, and then he shook my hand. My breath caught.

"That is a very interesting necklace, Ms. Ballentine."

"Rachel, please, and thank you." I disengaged my hand from his trying not to cringe. A slender man in his eighties, he exuded a cold ruthless energy that made me uncomfortable.

"May I?" he continued, motioning toward my neckline.

I felt Ed move closer, and I nodded. Dillingham touched the gold key and lifted it to turn it over, then rubbed his thumb over both sides. His unblinking reptilian eyes seemed to stare right through the key. He set it down. My heart skipped a beat, and my mouth went dry.

"Unusual," Old D murmured. "There is another fundraiser at the Masonic Auditorium next Saturday that you and Mr. Brogan here may not want to miss. I do hope that you will attend."

He was still staring at my neck, and the vision of fangs behind his closed grimace came to mind. Pushing the image aside, I asked," And who would we be helping?"

"Families who've recently lost their homes and need shelter." His eyes never left the key nestled above my chest.

"A worthy cause," I said, taking Ed's hand. "We'll try to make it." I said goodbye, and we walked away.

"Why'd you say we might go?" Ed whispered, as soon as we were out of earshot.

"Did you see how he stared at my chest?"

"Yes, I didn't enjoy that."

"He was fascinated by the key. He felt for the scratches. We have to go."

"Way too dangerous, Rachel."

"He wants us there. He's evil. There's black all around him. I just know Old D's involved in hurting Oliver. Going might tell us something."

"I don't know…"

"How's the camera working?" I asked, changing the subject.

Ed stared at me, and sighed. "Let's get something to eat." He then directed me toward the lavish display. Mounds of caviar, seafood, and every possible culinary delight greeted us. Moments later we sat at an empty table. I kicked off my shoes and wiggled my toes in the grass. "Ahhh." At his questioning look I explained. "No shoes." And then I dug into the plate of antipasto in front of me.

"Ed, could you hold a few things for me in your pockets?" I asked when I finished eating. He nodded, and I gave him the contents of my evening bag and slipped my shoes back on. I felt Ed's eyes on me as I walked toward the dessert table.

We left the party shortly thereafter.

Cookies for Oliver filling my purse.

• • •

The following afternoon, Ed and I sat in Oliver's den. Phil paced beside me swinging his pocket watch in sync to his steps as William unwrapped another peppermint, and Oliver opened a tin of cookies and shook his head. I'd recounted the prior evening's event, and expressed my desire to attend the charity function Dillingham mentioned. My grey panthers were not pleased. Neither was Ed. Sighing, I pulled the gold key from my pocket and turned it over and over in my hands.

William adjusted his suspenders over his red sweater, and reached across the coffee table. "I'll take that, young lady," he said, plucking the key from my hands. "This goes in the office safe."

"Yes, sir." I ducked out of the way of Phil's pocket watch.

"No." Oliver took another cookie from the tin.

"Oliver, you were the one who gave me *The Art of War.*"

"So you could learn litigation tactics, Rachel, not warfare."

"Well, we're in a war, and all warfare is based on deception. Sun Tzu taught warriors to keep your friends close, and your enemies closer. We need to get close."

"This is what you give her?" Ed said.

"For litigation. Not to wage war," Oliver defended.

"You know how things get with her," Ed said, scowling.

"Hello there, I'm here," I said, waving my arms about. "Can we get back to the Masonic party? We could go and casually bump into the Dillinghams, the Sun Tzu deception. We might learn something."

"Learn what? We don't have any evidence the Dillinghams are involved," William pointed out, unwrapping another peppermint.

"He was staring at the key," I said.

"Maybe he was just staring at your chest," Phil said, swinging his watch faster.

"What about rubbing the key for the scratches?"

"Or getting his hands near your chest, and is a dirty old man," Phil said.

His watch grazed my arm and I grabbed it.

"Phil, you're going to poke someone's eye out! Look, we'd just be attending a charity function. And we'd go straight from the car inside. They'll likely be plenty of security."

"Well..." William trailed off.

I sensed weakness and pressed. "What if my hunch is right? It's a calculated risk. The danger of going is worth it to find out more. Besides, you guys know my hunches."

"That's the problem...You'll stick to Ed like glue," Phil said, and I nodded. "All right. I vote go. I don't like it, but all right."

Ed, Oliver, and William were not happy, but eventually came around.

• • •

We'd just finished walking the indoor labyrinth at Grace Cathedral, and I really wanted to check out the Masonic Auditorium across the street. Taking Ed's hand, I asked if we could.

He nodded and we left the building, walking to the corner of California Street. There we waited for a cable car to pass. I looked up at the four large sculptures on the east end of the white building across the street, and recalled Oliver saying the smaller figures beside them depicted the struggle between the forces of good and evil.

"Why do you want to look at the auditorium?" Ed said, as we crossed and veered toward the imposing structure.

"Master Sun Tzu taught warriors to scope out enemy territory before the attack."

"We're just going to a party, Rachel."

"Sure, Ed." But I knew that this wasn't just any old building. The Masonic Temple, as it was commonly known, was the largest such auditorium in Northern California. As we walked up the portico steps to the main level, I noticed the Masonic square and compass architectural symbol prominently displayed on the wall. At the entrance I discovered an enormous mosaic dominating the entry foyer. Letting go of Ed's hand, I tried to pull open the glass door so I could get a better look.

"It's locked. Can we go now?" Ed asked.

"In a minute." I cupped my hands and peered inside. There were a number of etchings in the mosaic, double spirals, and the number eight. No, infinity ellipses, which seemed to be in patterns of three also embedded in the floor.

Unable to see anymore I said, "Let's go."

•   •   •

As soon as we returned home, I dashed into my office. Oliver had said the number eight and its connection to infinity came from the Templars, so I sifted through my stack of files until I found the one labeled *Templars*. I sat down and began to read:

After the First Crusade captured Jerusalem from Muslim Rule in 1099, a monastic order was created to protect Christian pilgrims traveling to visit the Holy Land. Jerusalem's King Baldwin II gave the order space in the captured Al Aqsa Mosque on Jerusalem's Temple Mount for their headquarters, a site steeped in mystique because it was built on top of the ruins of the original Temple of Solomon. Not surprisingly, most Templar legends stemmed from the knights' early occupation of the Temple Mount, and speculation about what relics they may have found there. Some claimed they found the Holy Grail while others alleged it was the Ark of the Covenant, fictions most scholars believed began circulating in the twelfth and thirteenth centuries.

Once the church formally blessed the impoverished order, they soon became a favored charity entrusted with ample resources. The Templar Order was given control of great wealth and management of estates of noblemen participating in the Crusades, leaving most members holding noncombative positions to manage their vast financial infrastructure. Like a bank, they charged for these services, and Church decree exempted them from all taxes. However, by the mid-1100s, Jerusalem was recaptured forcing the Templars to relocate, and by 1303, the Crusaders had lost their last foothold in the Holy Land. This ended the Templars' military mission, but left their two hundred years of financial tentacles throughout the Christian empire. It also left King Philip IV of France deeply in debt to the Templars. So when Pope Clement V asked him to investigate false charges made by an ousted Templar, the king seized on the opportunity.

I'd just read how the Templars were connected to the Friday the thirteenth superstition when I heard Ed call, "Rachel, dinner."

"This looks wonderful," I said when I joined him moments later. Eggplant parmigiana was my favorite.

"So what have you been up to?" he asked, watching me dig in.

"Yum," I said, and he smiled. "Well, do you know the origins of the Friday the thirteenth superstition?" Ed shook his head, so I told him about the Templars and King Philip's debt.

"No bankruptcy court?"

"Funny. No, his method was a bit more grisly—he tortured his creditors."

"I don't think the Visa people would like that."

"Too bad," I said, and explained that on Friday, October 13, 1307, King Philip ordered French Templars arrested for heresy, and extracted false confessions by torturing them. He then burned them at the stake based on these coerced confessions and threatened the Pope with war unless he also arrested the Templars.

"Which the Pope did."

"Yep. The surviving Templars fled."

"Where'd they go?" Ed asked.

"A lot of them went to Scotland because it wasn't controlled by the Church. I think the Templars hooked up with the masons there and started Freemasonry back in the 1300s. And I also think Prince Henry Sinclair helped them sail to America."

"Okay, enough," Ed said.

"Sorry, I just love all this stuff."

"I know. But right now I need you to focus your attention on me."

I looked at Ed. Was I neglecting him? I have been preoccupied. I set my fork down. "Did you know that eggplant parmigiana tastes a gazillion times better reheated?" Standing, I walked around the table and held out my hand.

An hour later we reheated our dinner, and it really did taste better.

CHAPTER 15

There were two octagon houses in San Francisco. Both eight-sided homes were built in the late 1800s, and listed on the National Register of Historic Places. The McElroy Octagon House on Gough Street housed a museum and was open to the public. The Feusier Octagon House, on Green Street in Russian Hill, was a private residence. The owners were friends of Phil and Lynn and where we were to head in case of trouble. Of course, when Ed told me about it I thought earthquake, never imagining I'd be seeking refuge there this evening.

I'd gotten home from work, changed into jeans, and gone upstairs to visit Oliver. I found him in his den watching a documentary on the golden ratio. Joining him I learned snowflakes, crystals, even the proportions of a bird's body to its wings, shared the same mathematical ratio.

"The Templars used the golden ratio when constructing buildings," Oliver said when the program was over.

"Really?"

"Templars, Masons, even the architects of the Great Pyramid. The same patterns extend throughout the universe. Some people believe there's a master architect at work."

"A divine plan. Makes you wonder about the possibility of a higher power," I said just as my cell phone rang. "Hey darling, I'm running late. Could you meet me at Caesar's on Bay Street at *the* eight, sweetheart? Honey bear?" Ed asked, his tone syrupy sweet.

What? We never spoke to each other like that. And he'd said *the* eight. Something was wrong. Very wrong, and we needed to leave. Oliver's bodyguard, Wayne, hadn't yet arrived, and we were all alone. Trying not to panic I said, "Okay, pumpkin. *The* eight, it is sweetie. Bye, honey bear," and hung up.

"Oliver, get your coat. We're leaving. Now!"

"What?" He furrowed his brow. He'd been engrossed in the six o'clock news.

"No time to explain. Just trust me."

Oliver nodded. He slipped on his shoes and walked into the hallway to grab his coat. I plopped a hat on his head, and then we rode downstairs in the service elevator to the garage. "No talking," I whispered. I took his hand and led him out the side exit. I didn't see anyone, so I ushered Oliver through our neighbor's property. From there we quickly walked the six blocks to "the eight."

My fingers shook as I entered the security code on the panel next to the side entrance gate. When I heard a click, I pushed the door ajar and pulled a silent Oliver with me. Metal banged like a gunshot when I shut the door. I flinched. We then walked toward the backyard. Sitting on a wooden bench hidden in shadows, we waited for Ed. Ten minutes later he joined us. He looked about before taking my hand and led us to the house. I didn't even realize I was still holding on to Oliver.

Once inside, Ed headed to the kitchen and punched in a code on the keypad adjacent to its entry. A concealed door sprung open. We walked through it. The door slowly closed behind us, and a light came on revealing a narrow windowless passage built at a sharp downward incline. It led to an octagon-shaped room made of concrete approximately fifteen by fifteen feet at its widest point.

"What is this?" Oliver murmured, looking about.

"A bomb shelter," Ed said.

"I can't believe this is here," Oliver whispered.

"You okay, Oliver?" I inquired as we sat on a small sofa. When he said he was fine, I turned back to Ed. "So, what's the blasted emergency?"

"You know we put cameras and bugs in your lobby." I nodded, and he continued. "Now Rachel, don't get mad, but I also bugged your place."

"What?" I yelled.

"Sorry, babe, but I want to keep you safe."

"How could you do that without telling me?" I jumped up, balling my hands on my hips. "Why didn't you tell me? Wait—were we being taped when..." Oliver looked at me then and I knew I was turning red. *Crap*, I thought, touching my flaming cheeks. This just gets better, and better.

"Rachel, just listen," Ed said.

"I will not listen." I glared at Ed.

"Rachel." A muscle clenched in his jaw. "Just listen," Ed said again.

"Fine, go ahead." I crossed my arms in front of me.

"The new doorman let someone in to search your place."

"What?" I yelled.

"Calm down."

"Calm down! I will not calm down! You just told me someone searched my home, and I'm supposed to calm down. He touched my things." And then I felt my emotions shift and tears start to well.

"Rachel honey, don't cry." Ed pulled me into his arms.

"They searched my apartment?" I said, into his chest.

"You wore the key, babe. Their entry triggered the silent alarm, and I was able to watch them."

"Them?" Oliver said, and Ed told us the doorman let two men in.

"Two," I repeated, dismayed.

"Yeah, two. I haven't seen them before, but we have them on tape."

"When did they search?" I asked, calmer but still holding on to Ed. He said he called while the men were there, afraid they might go upstairs. They didn't, and John was at Oliver's now. Ed was also having one of his guys sweep my place to make sure they didn't plant any bugs. Sighing, I hugged Ed and told him I forgave him.

"But don't ever do anything like that again, or you'll be singing soprano for a week, mister," I warned.

Oliver laughed, and Ed gave him a dirty look.

"So what's next?" I asked.

"I'm going to check into the doorman and his accomplices," he said.

Oliver then asked why they didn't notice the alarm or surveillance equipment.

"They weren't looking for it," Ed told us, and phoned John. "No bugs—let's go."

Oliver and I followed Ed to his car and hid beneath a blanket in the back seat. Moments later, Ed drove into our garage. We waited ten minutes for Ed to get the doorman upstairs to view a supposed leak in my unit before we got out and ran toward the service elevator. John was waiting for us when the doors opened on Oliver's floor, and Wayne was back at his post.

"Seems there's been a bit of excitement," Wayne said and helped Oliver with his coat. Looking weary, Oliver told us he was turning in, and John escorted me downstairs.

It didn't look like anyone had searched my home, but I felt violated. I walked straight into the bedroom and stripped off all the bedding, and dumped the contents of my dresser on the floor. Ed stood by the doorway watching me. I picked up the linens and threw them in the stackable washer in the hallway, and went into the kitchen for cleaning supplies.

"Rachel?" Ed looked worried.

"They touched our things. I need to clean them." I knew I was acting a little crazy, but I couldn't help it.

Ed wrapped his arms around me and rested his chin atop my head. "Okay, babe."

The sun was rising when I tossed in the last load.

CHAPTER 16

The charity event was being held in the grand two-story lobby of the Masonic Auditorium. Spotlights shone down on the hundreds of guests wearing ball gowns and tuxedos. A few small tables were placed around the perimeter for informal seating, and a string quartet softly played off to the right. Waiters carrying champagne flutes circulated, and white-gloved attendants served artful hors d'oeuvres at a station on the left.

We'd arrived with John almost an hour ago. Ed wanted backup. I'd worn my new green silk dress, and Lynn had insisted I wear gold high-heeled torture devices she called shoes with it. My feet were killing me, and I really needed to sit down. I was about to tell Ed when I noticed Old D talking to one of the waitstaff. I'd spent the last hour scanning the crowd for him. As if sensing my stare, he looked up and gazed at my chest, and that disturbing feeling between my shoulder blades returned. Spooked, I instinctively placed my hand on Ed's arm.

"What?" he asked, eyeing me.

"Something's wrong."

"I know." Ed motioned to John who crossed the lobby to join us.

"Muddy boots, west exit. He hasn't moved in ten minutes," Ed said.

"There's another lookout by the stairs," John said.

"That's it, we're leaving." Ed asked John to get the car.

"Five minutes, Jones Street, side exit." John walked away.

And then someone screamed, "He's got a gun," and panic erupted. The music stopped and the din of the crowd died down. Ed grabbed my hand as several armed men wearing dark ski masks moved around the perimeter of the lobby blocking the exits. One strode to the center and fired a shot in the air. Amid the screams he yelled, "Quiet, all jewelry and wallets in the bags. Now!" He nodded at his cohorts, who distributed large sacks to the staff to circulate. An elderly woman next to us crumpled, and Ed reached out to cushion her fall.

When a waiter stood before us, I watched Ed place his wallet and watch in the bag. Terrified, I removed my earrings and then froze. I didn't want to hand over my engagement ring. It had belonged to Ed's grandmother. And I certainly didn't want to lose the key.

"Lady, you've got ten seconds to hand everything over or I'll kill him," a nearby gunman said, raising his weapon and pointing it at Ed's head. "Ten, nine, eight, seven," he started counting.

"Stop!" I shouted, startled out of my stupor.

Ed looked at me with beseeching eyes. "All right, all right," I mumbled, as I moved the key to the back of my neck while reaching around to open the clasp. I then tucked the key and my engagement ring into my uplifted hair, pretending difficulty with the clasp. When the robber raised his gun again, I dropped my necklace and earrings into the bag, my heart thundering long after he lowered his weapon. Ed took my hand and laced his fingers through mine, but I couldn't stop trembling.

Once they filled the sacks, the gunmen ordered us to lie facedown on the cold marble floor. I started shivering. I could hear people crying, and the woman beside me whimpering. The fear was tangible as we lay on the ground. Another shot rang out, followed by the instruction not to move. I saw boots walk by me and heard the sounds of receding footsteps. A moment later they were gone.

It seemed like forever before I heard the distant cry of sirens.

When the police arrived, they found everyone still lying on the floor. Thankfully, no one had been hurt. After giving an officer our statements, we walked over to John, and he asked if we were okay.

Ed said, "Yes," as a man holding a microphone offered his apologies for the evening's incident and any assistance he and his staff could provide. We then joined the folks leaving. As we neared the exit, I saw Old D looking on. His expression seemed oddly calm, even satisfied, and not shaky and frightened like the rest of us. Understanding surfaced, and I stumbled. He staged this robbery to get the key. Afraid, I turned and let him see my fear.

"Rachel," Ed warned, pulling me with him.

"Pretend weakness and encourage his arrogance. It will soon be his defeat, taught Master Sun Tzu."

Ed stopped and stared at me, and I looked away. I then followed him to the side entrance to wait for John to pick us up.

"That was not fun," John said, as we drove away.

"You just had to wear that necklace," Ed muttered.

"Hey, don't blame me. Dillingham committed armed robbery." I was about to tell them I'd saved the key when John said, "You think he staged the robbery to get the key?"

"A hundred percent. He wasn't scared like everyone else."

"Whatever, we need to reassess," Ed said.

"Well..." John paused.

"Well what?" Ed said.

"Well, I had some new tech, and it seemed like we might need it here, so I put a tracker on a twenty."

"You put... Awesome!"

"What are you two talking about?" I asked, and John explained that he'd slipped an ultrathin tracking device on a bill in his wallet before placing it in the bag. It was undetectable, and a satellite signal would allow us to follow the transmitter and trace its movement.

"Why would you possibly have that with you?" I was really starting to wonder about him.

"I like to test new equipment and stay on top of things," he said. "The appropriate response would be great job."

"Great job."

I definitely needed to find him a girlfriend.

•   •   •

As soon as we entered my apartment, Ed and John got busy tracking the money. I phoned Oliver, Phil, and William, and assured them we were all right. I then changed into sweats and went into my office. Staring out the window at the dark night sky, I touched my throat where my necklace had been, angry that I'd had no choice but to give them my jewelry. Well, most of it. There was no way I was handing over my engagement ring. It would have been worth getting shot to keep it. Irrational, I know, but how I felt. Ed would get over being mad once he saw his grandmother's ring.

Sighing, I took a seat. I was missing something. Old D staged the robbery to get the key. That I was sure of. So, what was so valuable about the key? The microchip? No, that didn't feel right. Old D must suspect that we'd found it. So again, what was so valuable about this key? There had to be something. I sorted through the files on my desk until I found the one labeled "Dr. Feden," and opened it. Dr. Feden had only taken magnified pictures of the key, and decoded the microchip. There wasn't any information on the actual key. Why would there be? No one cared about a house key. A tingling sensation enveloped me, and I smiled.

"Steganography," I said, and picked up Master Sun Tzu's inspired words. Flipping to a blank back page, I penned: "Spy Handbook Rule 1- Steganography."

"Did you say something?" Ed asked from the doorway.

"I need to show you something." I removed my engagement ring from my pocket and put it back on. "They were not getting my ring!"

He looked at my hand. "Rachel, they could have killed you."

"Ed, get mad at me later. I have something else I need to show you." I picked up the Dr. Feden file and handed it to him. "What's missing?"

"What?"

"You heard me, what's missing?"

Ed stared blankly at the file. "I'm not in the mood for games, Rachel."

"Fine. He only magnified the key. He never x-rayed it, or tested it. They were after the key, but not for the microchip," I said.

"I'm listening."

"We never looked for another message hidden within the key once we found the embedded computer chip. Steganography, Ed." I then pulled the duplicate key from my hair and held it out to him.

"How..." he started to ask, but changed his mind. Instead, he took the key from me and walked out of the room. A moment later I overheard him call Dr. Feden and ask him to examine the key. He still had the original.

We slept in and were in bed watching a Sunday morning news report on last night's robbery when Dr. Feden called. "What's up, George?" Ed asked, and hit speakerphone.

"You were right. The x-rays show a slender intricate object inside the key."

"Anything else?" Ed asked.

"Yes. The key is composed of a mixture of gold and titanium, and its weight is slightly heavier than a regular key. None of this was noticeable unless you were looking."

"Can you remove the object?"

"Only by destroying the metal around it. What do you want me to do?"

"Do it," Ed directed.

"It'll take a few days. I do have to say that the mixture of the gold and titanium metals is unusual. The strength and protection of the titanium I understand, but not the use of actual gold."

Since everything about the key was peculiar, I had to wonder at his surprise.

CHAPTER 17

I joined Oliver on the swings after dinner, excited to share Dr. Feden's discovery.

"A key within a key," Oliver said. "Incredible."

"The most obvious place is always the best place."

"It sure was. We all missed it."

"You didn't. You kept telling me to remember the key."

"Yes. Can we talk about that?" Oliver asked.

"Absolutely." I'd been waiting for him to bring up his out-of-body experience again. Oliver then told me he was still trying to remember everything, and had started writing down what he could recall in a notebook.

"Great idea. Hey, Oliver, have you ever heard of string theory?"

When he said he hadn't I explained that there were physicists who believe everything that exists is made up of energy and the vibration stemming from the movement of that energy, strings of energy vibrating in lines. According to the theory, a person's thoughts are also energy.

"So when you were unconscious, you sent out your energy strings—your signal. Since I'm open to it, like an antenna, I heard."

"Sounds absurd," Oliver said.

"Well, how else do you explain my hearing you when you were unconscious?"

"You're crazy."

"Oliver, be serious."

"I am serious. You're nuts, and even though you're nuts, you're smart. You knew about the key, and your subconscious deduced it had to be the answer."

"That wouldn't explain your part, and what you remember," I said.

"Maybe I was dreaming?"

"Do you really believe that Oliver?" I stopped midswing.

"I'm really not sure what to believe any more."

"Fair enough. I copied a bunch of articles on string theory that you might find of interest. They're on the hall table."

Oliver nodded, and I resumed swinging. When he started getting tired, I wished him good night, and headed downstairs.

• • •

I visited Oliver after work on Monday and found a file in the hallway. "Red?"

"No, crimson—for crazy."

"Oliver, there are noted physicists who believe in string theory, not just wackadoos."

"Wackadoos? Anyway, I need proof. The material was all theory." He walked into the living room.

"Fine, proof. I had a feeling you might be skeptical, so I came up with a new game for us." I joined him on the swings.

"I'm listening."

"I believe we're on the same wavelength, tuning into the same frequency like the radio. So we need to conduct a test like the FCC." I then suggested that before we go to sleep we each draw a picture of something in a notebook, and envision sending the picture to the other.

"Why?"

"Because we'll be testing the theory that thought is composed of energy vibrations which others can hear. It'll be a real scientific experiment, Oliver. C'mon, what do you say?"

"You're nuts."

"It could be fun."

"If I don't say yes, you'll wear me down, so fine." Oliver sighed.

"Great. Now remember, I'll also be sending you a picture. If you recall anything in the morning, just write it down. How about we compare notes in say two weeks?"

Oliver nodded, and we continued swinging. That evening I sent Oliver a picture of a bright golden daffodil. I awoke craving chocolate chip cookies—Oliver's favorite food. Not too original. I jotted it down.

On the way to the bathroom, an idea occurred to me, and I smiled.

Time to have some fun.

•   •   •

Five minutes later, I walked into the kitchen and poured a mug of coffee. Ed was on the phone. "You're kidding," he said, and quickly ended the call.

"What's up?" I took a seat.

"Oh nothing, just a little surveillance."

"What surveillance?"

"We've been following John's tracker on the twenty. It stopped in Mill Valley."

"Mill Valley—Dillingham's house!"

"You got it."

CHAPTER 18

D
r. Feden returned to Ed's house the following evening. He kept smiling. Once seated in Ed's den, he removed a small box and a file from his briefcase. He then opened the box and took out an old-fashioned ornate skeleton key, and placed it in Ed's hand. "The real key."

I looked at it, and was at a loss. The top was pretty with its three intersecting infinity loops, the same design as the inlaid floor pattern in the lobby of the Masonic Auditorium, but otherwise didn't appear out of the ordinary.

Dr. Feden stared at the key. "It's composed of an unknown metal that's lighter and stronger than any yet discovered."

"This key is made of a substance that doesn't exist?" Ed said, frowning.

"Yes. It is ten times stronger than steel, and its molecular structure is extraordinary," Dr. Feden confirmed.

"Molecular structure? You lost me," I said, sitting back.

"Okay, let's start with nanotechnology—the manipulation of matter on an atomic scale." He told us that one nanometer equals one billionth of a meter, which was like comparing a marble to the size of the earth. And atoms, the building blocks for all matter in the universe, have a diameter of about a tenth of a nanometer or one tenth of that marble.

"So, invisible," Ed said.

"Almost." Dr. Feden then explained that with today's

technology we can see them. Scientists had been working with nano-size structures to arrange sheets of carbon atoms and roll them into a tube, a nano-size cylinder of carbon atoms labeled a carbon nanotube. It had been theorized that even though all carbon nanotubes are made of carbon, they could be very different from one another based on how you aligned the individual atoms. Rolling the sheet side in different directions could theoretically create a carbon nanotube hundreds of times stronger than steel, but six times lighter.

"And this?" Ed said, looking at the key in his hand.

"Is the result," Dr. Feden finished with reverence.

"So it's priceless. Buildings, cars, airplanes could be made of it," Ed said with awe.

Wow! No wonder Dillingham would stop at nothing to get it back. But wait, what about Dr. Feden. How did we know we can trust him?

"I can read your mind, Rachel. I'm quite well-off, and I'd never steal from Ed."

I looked at Ed, and he nodded yes. If Ed trusted him, so did I. Shrugging I said, "Sorry."

"It's okay. Look at the key again. Do you see anything else?"

We both stared at the key. I shook my head.

"You're not supposed to. I went deeper, to the atomic level."

"And?" Ed asked.

"I found etchings on the key."

"Steganography!"

Dr. Feden smiled. "Yes, Rachel, steganography. There was a hidden message on the shaft of the object at the atomic level."

"What did it say?" I asked, moving forward in my seat.

"It looks like the lower case letters *a*, then *t*, then *x*, followed by an *n*, along with a symbol similar to the three intersecting infinity loops of the key. I didn't have time to look it up, but I believe it's either Latin or Greek." He then handed Ed a sheet of paper. Ed looked at it and shrugged, and passed it to me.

"I don't think that's an *n*. It looks like a fancy upside down letter *u*, which is the symbol for omega in the Greek alphabet." At Ed's questioning look I said, "*Star Trek*," and told them about an episode where the *Enterprise* was beamed to the distant planet Omega IV, and the symbol decorated their flag. I then turned toward Dr. Feden. "I'm a bit confused. What's the real significance of all of this?"

"In principle, if we could learn to rearrange atoms, then the possibilities are limitless. If we can rearrange the atoms in coal, we can make a diamond. If we rearrange the atoms in water, we can make wine."

"So if whoever created this understands how to put atoms together on a nanoscale, they could potentially arrange atoms to create anything?" I said.

"Yes, exactly, anything," Dr. Feden said.

The implications were astounding. No famines or droughts, and the possible medical uses.

"Unbelievable," Ed said.

"This is just like the Replicator," I said, feeling stunned.

"Replicator?" Dr. Feden inquired as his right brow lifted.

"On *Star Trek*." At his blank look I asked, "You've never watched *Star Trek*?" He shook his head, and I wondered how that could be. He was a scientist.

"Rachel," Ed warned.

"Fine, whatever," I said, and told Dr. Feden that the Replicator was the name of a machine on the original television program *Star Trek* that could make anything. You just typed in or said what you wanted, and it would magically recreate it by rearranging air molecules.

"Interesting." He turned to speak to Ed. As they talked, I tried to recall where I'd seen that symbol before. And then I heard *remember the key* once again. Okay, the key, the microchip, the coin… The coin!

"Thank you."

"Thank you for what, Rachel?" Ed asked.

"I can't believe we all forgot. Hold on." I retrieved my key chain with the attached USB drive and plugged it into Ed's laptop. "Look." I pointed at the screen. The etched symbol was engraved on the lower left of the backside of the coin from the decoded microchip.

"I did forget," Ed admitted.

"And I was distracted trying to date the key," Dr. Feden said.

"Oh, like carbon dating?" I asked.

"Not exactly. Carbon is used for dating organic matter like plants or people. I used thermoluminescense dating, or TL, which measures the accumulated radiation dose to date inorganic matter."

"You know how to do that? I'm impressed."

"I'm a physicist. I only dabble with computer encryption."

Dabble? Was he kidding me?

Dr. Feden said he'd cashed in a few favors and was able to use the large lab in Berkeley by the university. His data showed the key was about twelve thousand years old, but warned he could be way off because it was made of an unknown substance, and possibly manipulated, since whoever made it might know how to arrange atoms.

"Did you just say twelve thousand years old?" Ed asked, and Dr. Feden nodded.

"Wow! 10,000 BC. That's the Stone Age." Saber-toothed tigers and woolly mammoths appeared in my mind.

"It's science fiction." Ed shook his head and sat back.

"Yes, but a very real possibility," Dr. Feden said, and left shortly thereafter.

Ed and I remained seated in the den. I felt dazed and excited at the same time. I took the key from Ed and stared at it.

"Can you believe this?" I asked, awed.

Ed stood and retrieved his laptop and a pad. He sat beside me and Googled the Greek alphabet. Then we compared the letters on the sheet Dr. Feden gave us.

"You were right, that is the symbol for omega. It means great."

"Yes, but look. It's also the last letter in the Greek alphabet," I said.

"Does that help?"

"I don't know. I'm just pointing it out."

"Okay." Ed grabbed a pen and we started translating. Once done he handed me the pad: "*a,t,x,n:* Alpha Tau Chi Omega."

"I am the alpha and omega, the beginning and the end, the first and the last."

"Huh?"

"New Testament Book of Revelation," Ed said.

"It's all Greek to me."

"That was horrible, Rachel."

"Sorry, I had to say it," I said, hands held up in surrender. I then looked at the pad once more. "Ed, this is absolutely amazing."

"I agree. The question is what do we do with it?"

"I don't know...yet."

CHAPTER 19

Ed was hiding something. The feeling surfaced right after John's tracker stopped at Dillingham's house. That was four days ago, and when I asked Ed what he was hiding, he said I was being ridiculous. Ridiculous my foot. He was up to something.

The following morning, Ed asked everybody to meet him at Oliver's penthouse later that afternoon. Phil brought Lynn, and William arrived with John. Once everyone was seated in the den, Ed told us that he'd *recovered* the tracker from Dillingham's home.

"What? Young man that's breaking and entering," William said, his tone appalled.

"I know sir, but it was the only way. We didn't steal anything, just left a surveillance camera and tapped his phones."

"What?" William's face reddened.

Ed knew we couldn't be held as accomplices if we didn't know what he was up to. I didn't like that he'd hid this from me, but I understood.

"Calm down," Phil said, and told me to get William a drink. I removed a tin of cookies from the liquor cabinet and handed them to Oliver, and then poured William a scotch. William was a stickler with rules. Phil was more pragmatic—everything wasn't black and white, and sometimes you needed to work in the grey. I agreed with Phil. I gave William his scotch and sat next to Ed on the sofa.

"I made sure there's no evidence we were ever there," Ed added.

"'Deception is crucial,' instructed Master Sun Tzu."

William glared at me.

"Well, he broke into my apartment. Now we're even." I squeezed Ed's hand and sat back.

William's responding silence was deafening.

Phil started pacing and jingling the coins in his pockets. When he pulled out his pocket watch, I grabbed it, and gave it to Lynn.

Phil frowned and turned to Ed. "Did you get anything useful?"

Ed moved his laptop aside and opened the folder he'd brought with us.

"We can't use that," William said.

"Well, not in court, but..." Phil shrugged.

"I focused on the room where the tracking signal stopped. These were taken with an infrared camera, so the lighting may seem a bit off." Ed spread photographs showing a 360-degree circle of the room on the coffee table. I gasped when I saw the room's massive wooden door with the key's infinity loop symbol carved into it.

"I left the surveillance camera there for a few days. Check this out," Ed said, and switched on his laptop. Seconds later the screen showed the photographed room, dark except for slivers of moonlight seeping through the shuttered windows. Then a sound. The door opened and Old D walked in wearing a bathrobe. He turned on the lights. He then crossed the room and pushed something on the back wall. A panel lifted revealing a safe with an electronic keypad. He entered a code. Something clicked, and the door cracked open. Old D pulled out a box, and placed it on the table behind him. Picking up a phone, he took a seat.

"It's been sorted. We didn't get it...I'm sure it's the one. The little bitch hid it somewhere." He laughed, and then loudly coughed. "I'm fine," he gasped. He listened a moment. "Son, you may do with her as you wish once I have the key." He slammed the receiver down.

Old D pulled out a thick stack of bills, and returned the box to the safe. Two minutes later, he'd shut the lights and closed the door behind him.

Ed stopped the video.

"Well, now we know Dillingham is behind the robbery," I said.

"And probably Oliver's shooting. But why is the symbol from the key and the coin engraved on his door?" Phil asked already pacing.

"Good question," Oliver said.

"And did you hear him call me a bitch?"

"Kiddo, do you really care what he thinks of you?" Oliver said.

"I guess not. It was just really uncalled for, that's all."

Ed then asked if anyone noticed the small prescription bottle by the telephone. When no one responded, he held up an enlarged picture of the bottle. Vasotec. Ed told us it was the leading medication for patients with heart disease and could explain why Dillingham was always coughing.

"Sounds good." Phil paced faster. And then he stopped. "We have schematics for a coin, a key of unknown origin, and Dillingham's involved. How does it fit?"

"No idea. All we know is Dillingham wants the key, and he won't stop searching for it," I said.

"And thanks to Rachel they know we have it," Ed said.

"Hey! Because of me we also know Dillingham's involved."

"True, but we still don't know the connection between the coin and the hidden key, or even how John Bush got it." Phil jingled the coins in his pockets.

"It doesn't matter. The most important thing is that we're all safe," Oliver said.

"We need to get rid of it." William stood and walked over to the liquor cabinet. He poured another scotch.

"You're right. They're going to keep looking for the key. What if we give everything to Pete? He can do a broadcast and let the entire world know. Agreed?" Phil asked.

Everyone nodded and Phil pulled out his phone. I knew it was the right thing to do, I just wish we understood how everything fit. A few minutes later Phil told us that Pete was in New York. He'd be back next weekend, and would meet with us on Sunday with a camera crew.

With that settled I moved my hair aside and asked Lynn, "Do you like my new earrings?" Ed had surprised me with beautiful diamond studs to replace the ones stolen in the robbery.

"They're lovely. Two carats." I didn't question how Lynn knew that.

"Did you tell her?" John asked. He'd sat quietly near the door this entire time.

"Tell me what?"

"Nothing," Ed said, throwing John a dirty look.

"Ed?" My bullshit detector was going off. Noticing our attentive audience, I decided to question him when we were alone and he was in a more vulnerable position. Instead, I focused on John, certain the universe wanted me to help him.

"Hey John, speaking of your love life, we need to have Lynn take you shopping. These bland clothes don't do a thing for you." I looked at his dull brown shirt and loose beige khakis and cringed.

"I like them." John stood.

"Sure you do, sure you do," I agreed, hooking my arm through his. "But you're open-minded and amenable to improvement. I just know you are."

Meanwhile, Lynn had turned to stare at John and take inventory. I could feel him squirming. I also felt the taught muscles he tried so hard to hide.

"I think some rich chocolates and blues would be a good basic palette," Lynn said, and had John agreeing to join her shopping in under a minute. He fled right after.

I couldn't help it. I started laughing.

"You enjoyed that," Oliver said.

"Absolutely," I admitted.

"I thought you believed in karma—what goes around and all that."

"It's to help him, so it's good karma."

"If you say so, kiddo," Oliver said smiling. "If you say so."

CHAPTER 20

It was six in the morning, and I sat at the kitchen table sipping my third cup of coffee. I'd been unable to sleep, and had spent the last two hours re-reading my notes. I was thinking about what happened when people traded in their gold for dollars when Ed walked in.

"Morning," Ed said, interrupting my thoughts. He poured himself a cup, and took a seat.

"Morning. Ed, what if there was no gold in Fort Knox?"

"Excuse me?"

"What if there was no gold in Fort Knox?"

"I believe they check our reserves on a regular basis to ensure that it's there."

"But who checks it? The people who stole it? There were a lot of people back in the seventies and eighties who said the gold's already been looted. Wait a sec." I walked into my office. It took a few minutes to find what I wanted.

"Look at this." I pushed a dozen pages across the kitchen table.

"Can't I relax and read the paper first?"

I raised my brows in answer. Ed sighed and took the proffered sheets.

Shortly after FDR had Americans turn in their gold coins for dollars, claims that the gold had been looted surfaced. The allegations increased over the next few decades. By 1974, sufficient media pressure had been brought to bear so that the Director of the US Mint took six Congressmen, one Senator, and a few reporters, on a tour of Fort Knox. They visited one of the smallest vaults, and not the Central Core Vault in the basement. Visitors on that day noticed the gold had a strange orange color indicative of a high copper content, and not the .995 pure gold known as good delivery gold. A magnified photo of Representative Snyder of Arizona placing a gold bar on a US Postal scale revealed the bar weighed 22.25 pounds. A normal bar of .995 gold would weigh 28.9 pounds, and nearly 30 percent more. The Secretary of the Treasury unsuccessfully tried to explain away the discrepancy, and conclusion, that the little gold we had was diluted.

Subsequent reporters continued to allege that our nation's gold had probably been stolen, and that Fort Knox was likely empty. Recently, European newspapers were flooded with stories about a high-ranking French bureaucrat's claim he had proof the Fort Knox gold was gone.

"Well?" I asked when Ed looked up.

"Interesting. But there is that pesky problem of proving any of this."

"I know, I know. I just feel like I'm onto something. Ed, dear—"

"No!"

"I haven't said anything yet."

"It's what you're about to say that scares me."

Standing, I moved around the table and sat on his lap. "Ed, honey, do you have a Fort Knox guy?"

"No!"

"You said you have a guy for everything."

"Almost everything. Rachel, it's Fort Knox!"

"What about the security cameras? Could Geoffrey hack in and see what's going on?"

"Rachel, you're talking about the government. They toss you in prison and throw away the key for doing that."

"Maybe John? One of his contacts?"

"Fine, I'll ask, but don't get your hopes up. Now, can I read the paper?"

"Of course, dear. I love you." I returned to my seat to switch on the morning cartoons. The colorful antics of Bugs Bunny and Wile E. Coyote appeared.

"Great," he muttered, picking up *The Times.*

• • •

As soon as Ed left, I went into my office. While talking to him I'd remembered that snitches like the French official also had another name. Excited, I logged onto my computer and typed *whistleblower* into Nexlaw, the legal search engine, and discovered the False Claims Act (FCA).

Evidently, there were corrupt defense contractors even back during the American Civil War. They sold faulty rifles, rancid rations, and decrepit horses to the Union Army, and the Justice Department refused to prosecute them. Fed up, Congress enacted the FCA in 1863. It was based on the thirteenth century English Qui tam action, which let a person sue on the king's behalf when the king was wronged. Similarly, the FCA let a citizen sue folks swindling the US government when the Justice Department failed to go after them. These lawsuits were commonly referred to as Qui tam actions.

There were several highly publicized Qui tam actions against crooked government contractors for severe price gouging, and misuse of government property, in the 1980s. Congress responded by adding broad secrecy provisions to the FCA. So now if you wanted to snitch and file a Qui tam action, the court automatically sealed the lawsuit so no one could view it, and immediately issued a gag order against you forbidding you from speaking about it. The Justice Department then had sixty days to decide if it would prosecute, but could secretly request an open-ended extension that could freeze the lawsuit forever. Further, these extension requests were rubber stamped by a clerk and not reviewed by a judge.

It screamed corruption to me. The Justice Department could protect their cronies by deciding not to go after certain people. Since the whistleblower was barred from saying anything about it, no one would know. Challenging the gag provisions might provide a legal way to get those varmints, as my friend Yosemite Sam would say. But there was still that pesky problem of proof.

I printed the material on the FCA and then Googled Fort Knox. When FDR had everyone turn in their gold coins as part of the New Deal, he needed somewhere to put it. So in 1936, the US Treasury started building the Bullion Depository at Fort Knox, Kentucky, a fortified vault to store the nation's gold reserves. The Treasury Department had since expanded, and now included twelve bureaus. The Bureau of the Mint had custody and protected our nation's gold in several fortresses around the country, including San Francisco.

"That's right." I'd noticed the Mint building near the top of a hill. Homes and apartment buildings were built right across the street from it, and I'd thought it nonoperational. Shrugging, I Googled the Mint, and was immediately captivated by our city's history. When my phone rang, I jumped. It was William. A clerk would be delivering a box of files so I could work from home. With Dillingham's people still out there looking for the key, and five days until Uncle Pete arrived, I wasn't taking any unnecessary chances.

Hanging up, I placed my Mint research aside, and went through my e-mail messages. An hour later the clerk arrived. I opened my front door and found a *Young Frankenstein* DVD taped to it. Last night I'd sent Oliver the image of a mad scientist cackling with insane laughter as lightening thundered in the background for our FCC experiment.

"Very funny, Oliver," I murmured, removing it. I thanked the clerk for bringing the box, and returned to my office to attack my client files. Billable hours still paid my mortgage. I opened the Lewis folder, an acrimonious divorce involving millions in marital assets, and thanked the universe for Ed.

The day flew by. At six, I stopped and went into the kitchen and gathered the ingredients to make Oliver cookies. I truly believed in the curative powers of chocolate, and dumped mounds of chips into the bowl. Dozens of cookies cooled on racks all over the kitchen by the time Ed walked in. He snagged a warm cookie, mumbled "Yum," and gave me a kiss.

"I know better than to ask who these are for," he said, reaching for a second.

"So were you able to speak to Geoffrey about hacking into Fort Knox?"

"Yes, and he's considering it. I think you're both crazy."

"Yes, dear." I placed wax paper inside a colorful tin and turned to find Ed staring at me.

"You're up to something."

"I don't know what you're talking about."

"Don't play dumb, what's going on?"

"Nothing, dear. Have another cookie."

• • •

We were relaxing on the living room sofa after dinner when Geoffrey phoned. He and his girlfriend were on their way to Vegas to "do it."

"Ask him to also *do* the San Francisco Mint."

Ed looked curiously at me, but did as requested. As soon as he hung up I said, "Vegas?"

"What happens in Vegas stays in Vegas, and it's easier to be invisible there."

"And he has a girlfriend."

"Yes, Rachel, so leave him alone."

"I've no idea what you're talking about." I sat back and told him about the Treasury Bureaus. I then jumped into the California Gold Rush and the need to convert miners' gold into coins, which led to the opening of the San Francisco Mint in 1854. In 1874 it was moved to the Granite Lady, a bigger facility resembling an ancient Greek temple with huge columns. Designed to float on its foundation so it wouldn't shatter during a quake, the Mint, in fact, survived the 1906 earthquake practically undamaged. The only San Francisco financial institution able to open for business, it became a major depository, and by 1934, one-third of the United States gold reserve was stored in the vaults of the San Francisco Mint.

In response, the city built a larger Mint on Duboce Avenue, and all minting operations were transferred there in 1937. Constructed as a fortress, with gun towers, a network of pipes that could instantly flood the building with tear gas, and an electrically operated steel entrance door, its vaults had concrete walls several feet thick. Today, the Mint only produced proof coin sets, and commemorative coins Congress authorized. It also didn't allow visitors.

"And with your overactive imagination, no visitors means conspiracy," Ed concluded.

"You bet. They have their own Mint police so no one on the outside can see what they're up to on the inside. I read they even have a bike patrol to cycle around the perimeter."

"I know. Todd is one."

"You're kidding, your training partner? Call him!" I said.

"Why?"

"He'll know if there's anything fishy going on in there."

"Well, something has been bothering him lately," Ed said. "But who knows if it has anything to do with his job."

"Of course it does."

My angels always provided a way.

• • •

Ed phoned his friend and arranged to go for a run at six tomorrow morning. I'd never understood why people tortured themselves that way, and at that hour. At seven, two sweaty men joined me in the kitchen for morning coffee. Ed made the introductions and then told us he was going to take a shower.

As soon as he left, Todd said, "Ed told me you're a lawyer."

"Yes."

He took a seat and drummed his fingers on the table. Todd stared into his mug and finally looked up. "I'm sworn to secrecy about my job."

"I understand." I took a seat next to him.

"As my lawyer, anything we discuss you can't tell anyone. Correct?"

"Yes, that's the way privilege works."

A muscle clenched in his jaw, and I could hear his foot tapping under the table.

"Is there something you'd like to talk about with me? As your lawyer?"

Todd looked away and began drumming his fingers on the table again. I waited. The drumming stopped and Todd unzipped a jacket pocket. His hand shook as he reached inside. "Here," he said, pushing a gold coin across the table.

My heart skipped, and I wanted to scream with excitement. Slightly larger than a quarter, the word *liberty* in capital letters spanned the rounded top, and a raised imprint of America was depicted underneath. I picked up the coin and held it in my hand. Flipping it over, I saw a large script number one. Below it I read *AMERO* and saw the key's infinity loop symbol underneath. *AMERO* hadn't been on the microchip image. I set the coin down on the table and stared. Elation bubbled through me. The coin was real!

Ed walked in to get more coffee and froze. "Is that what I think it is?" He took a seat and picked up the coin. "Todd, how did you get this?"

"From Joe." He explained that Congress hadn't authorized any new coins in a while, so nothing should have been going on at the Mint. Yet a few weeks ago, activity started, and his team began asking questions. A lot of people were going in and out, and it made no sense. They were told it was a special edition and not to say anything. And then a new unit of security guards showed up.

"They don't usually do that?" I asked.

Todd shook his head. "They never do that. So our captain went to see what was going on. The next day he asked me to hold on to that for him." He pointed at the coin. He then told us that Joe, his captain, didn't show up to work the next day, and no one on his team had seen him since. They went by his apartment a few days later, and all of his things were gone.

I looked at Ed. They made a federal cop disappear. My excitement ebbed as my fear grew, and my mouth went dry. I cleared my throat. "Does anyone else know?"

"Our superior. He said Joe got a transfer to SRT, special response team, and had to leave immediately. He's lying. We're a tight group. Joe would have told us." I could hear his foot tapping under the table again.

"How'd Joe get the coin?" I asked.

"No idea. All I know is Joe vanished, there's a lot of people going in and out of the facility, and we're not allowed near anything. Oh, and there are trucks leaving the building in the middle of the night."

Trucks?

"Do you know where they go?" Ed asked.

When he didn't, Ed said he'd find out. I stared at him. *Hello—they got rid of a federal officer!*

"I just don't know what to do." Todd sighed and ran a hand over his cropped hair.

"I've an idea." I explained about being a whistleblower. Todd needed to think about it, but agreed to leave the coin with us for safekeeping. He'd known Ed for years and trusted him.

"This is crazy," I said after Todd left.

"I know. We found the coin."

"There are no coincidences, Ed."

Thank you, angels. You're welcome drifted back in response.

"Why am I always hearing 'you're welcome' around you," Ed mumbled, as his cell phone rang.

It was Geoffrey. He'd done *it*, and would be back from Vegas shortly.

"He's a dark horse," I commented once Ed hung up.

"People are rarely what they appear to be."

• • •

John arrived at noon with the external drive Geoffrey gave him. Ed plugged it into his laptop and said, "Give me a minute."

"Can you believe it?" I asked John, and started pacing, too excited to sit still. "Todd had the coin."

"Pretty incredible," John agreed, just as Ed told us he was ready. Ed then explained that Geoffrey tried to get into the gold audits by the Inspector General's Office, but there were a lot of firewalls, and he didn't want to hang around. So he made it look like the IRS was the real target because everyone hates them.

"The Sun Tzu deception," I said.

"I need to throw out that book. Anyway, Geoffrey sent Bush an IRS assessment of seven hundred billion dollars."

"You're kidding." Dark horse and a sense of humor.

"Hopefully everyone will think the hacks are a joke."

"Hold out bait to entice the enemy, feign disorder, and crush him, spoke Master Sun Tzu."

Ed ignored me, and said the folders on the right were the camera footage inside the Mint buildings. Geoffrey had copied everything rather than stick around viewing them for what we might have wanted. When John reminded him that we only needed the SF one because of what Todd had told us, Ed needed another moment. Shrugging, I turned toward John.

"So what's your tattoo of?"

"I don't..." He stopped when I tapped his wrist. I'd noticed traces of ink beneath his watch on a few occasions.

"Come on. If you show me yours, I'll show you mine."

Sighing, John removed his watch, and held his wrist out revealing a one-inch cross. Each of the four arms formed a "v" with two points.

"It's a Celtic cross. Legend says if you extend lines from each of the eight points it will go on forever. Now yours," he said.

I slipped my shirt off my right shoulder and turned so he could see the small pink angel watching my back.

"What is it with you two?" Ed asked, waiting for us.

I straightened my shirt and then watched the monitor displaying empty hallways and rooms of quiet equipment. Ed sped through the footage, but it was all the same. An hour later we stopped and looked at each other. All of the people and activity Todd mentioned was absent. The footage was faked. Someone was covering his tracks.

"We'll do the Mint tonight," I overheard Ed say while walking John out.

"What time?" I asked when Ed joined me in the kitchen.

"You're not going!"

We'd see about that. So I just shrugged. "Dinner will be ready in an hour. I'm going to Oliver's." I felt his eyes boring into my back as I walked away.

Once upstairs, I asked Oliver how he thought our FCC experiment was going. Oliver grinned, and I had to laugh. I then told him about John's tattoo.

"You did hear that his real name is Sinclair, which is Scottish. And the eight-pointed cross belonged to the Scottish Knights Templar." Oliver picked up a pad and drew an octagon with the Templar cross inside it. The points touched the angles of the octagon. He then drew lines away from the points on the octagon. "When you draw lines outward from the Newport Tower points, they lead you to what many believe are Templar land-claim markings that they've found."

"That's so amazing. What if we drew lines from the points of the eight-sided house? Where would they go?"

"Good question, kiddo. We'd need an aerial view and maybe a satellite map to figure it out."

"I'll leave that to you. I need to get going. And pace the cookies," I reminded as he reached for the tin.

"Sure, kiddo," he said and removed two.

CHAPTER 21

We drove toward the San Francisco Mint. Ed tightly gripped the steering wheel, and a muscle clenched in his jaw. He was mad at me. I'd threatened to rat him out to William if he didn't take me with him.

"Next time I'm tying you to the bed."

"Sounds like fun."

Ed frowned and kept driving. Moments later, he parked our dark sedan on the west side of the Mint near Grove Street. Lights shone in the windows of a handful of surrounding residences and apartment buildings. I looked across the street. A concrete-and-iron fence encircled the fortress, but a moat seemed more fitting.

"No talking, got it?" Ed said for the umpteenth time.

Sighing in irritation, I just nodded and pulled my navy ski hat lower. We then sprinted across the street to meet John. Dressed in dark clothing, he melded into the night.

Two hours later the Mint's metal gates opened, and the first of three trucks drove through. The lead truck turned, and then slowed, pausing at the stop sign on Buchanan Street. It then continued on. Another truck followed.

Ed moved closer to the stop sign. I stayed with John and anxiously watched the last truck slow to a stop at the sign. Ed rolled underneath to attach a tracking device. The truck drove on with Ed lying flat on the ground. He crawled back and joined us, and I felt myself breathe again.

John then motioned toward the side street where our vehicle was parked out of view. Ed grabbed my hand and we ran to the car. John was already behind the wheel starting the engine when Ed opened the back door and shoved me in. Twenty minutes later, we parked in Ed's garage. I removed my ski hat and followed the men inside.

"I still don't understand why you were such a pain about my coming," I said as Ed pulled out his cell phone. I knew he'd be calling Geoffrey. He pushed speakerphone, and I heard ringing.

"Well?" Ed said when Geoffrey answered.

"Working perfectly. They went over the Golden Gate and are heading north on 101. I'll keep you posted."

Geoffrey phoned about an hour later. The trucks had stopped at 20601 Bohemian Avenue in Monte Rio.

"Bohemian Grove?" John asked, and Ed nodded.

At my questioning look, Ed said the Bohemian Grove was a 2700-acre campground located seventy-five miles north of San Francisco. It belonged to a private men's group known as the Bohemian Club and just about every President and head of a major corporation has been a member. Steeped in wealth, power, and secrecy, the Club hosted a three-week private encampment of some of the most powerful men in the world each summer.

"Why would the trucks go there?" I asked.

"Good question. We need to get inside," Ed said, and looked at me. "You *can't* go."

"Well, why not?"

"Because it would be impossible to hide you. They don't allow women."

"What?"

"Rachel, it's a private club. They can discriminate."
Blast, he was right.

•   •   •

Ed called Phil at 7:00 a.m. and told him we were coming over for lunch. As soon as we arrived Phil asked, "What's up?"

"We might be able to drop a pin receiver on one of the drivers," Ed said, explaining that a powerful microphone one-quarter of the length of a sewing needle and about one-third as slender could be placed on a person's clothing and remain virtually undetectable. If discovered, it would look like a pin one found on dry-cleaned clothing, and only the savviest or those sweeping for surveillance equipment would realize it wasn't.

"I'm not sure how we'd get close enough though," Ed finished.

"I've an idea," I said, and they both looked at me.

"Why am I nervous?" Ed muttered.

Ignoring him I said, "I've watched gazillions…"

"Gazillions again, Rachel? That is not a word," Phil said.

"Yeesh, yes gazillions of spy movies, and they always use a hot chick to distract the men. I'm the hot chick." I stuck out my hip in a sexy pose.

"No." Phil shook his head.

"No," Ed repeated, wearing a stubborn expression.

"Listen, I could be a stranded motorist driving a beat-up old car with no signal on my phone. I'd ask them to look at my tire so I could get near one of them. I'm sure a wig and short shorts would do the trick!"

"I've a much better idea. Arthur's a member. He could take me in as a guest," Phil said. Arthur Towland was Lynn's brother. Phil had started the law firm of Brown and Towland with his brother-in-law over forty years ago, and Arthur, age seventy and recently retired, was a serious power broker.

"He's family. And he owes me, big time. He'll do it. I can also ask him to sponsor me for membership if need be."

"Especially since you're retired."

"Rachel," Phil warned, and Ed frowned.

Yeesh. These guys had no sense of humor.

• • •

Phil and William agreed to meet with us at Oliver's that evening. "Don't have a cow, just listen." I then told Oliver and William what had been going on over the last few days.

"What?" William roared.

"Are you crazy? Hacking into Fort Knox!" Oliver shouted.

"Calm down, Oliver."

"Rachel, I will not calm down." Oliver stood and waved his hands about. "This is all too dangerous. Don't you people remember—I was shot?"

"Of course we remember. But you need to listen," Phil said.

"You too, Phil?" Oliver glared at Phil and sat. He then splayed his left hand over his chest and scowled at all of us. I moved over and covered his right hand with mine. He shook it off.

"Please, Oliver," I said.

"Fine, just say whatever you have to," he snapped.

I glanced at William and didn't like how flushed and red he was getting. I got up and poured him a scotch and handed it to him. He drank it in one gulp and held out the glass for another. Not good.

"Ed, your turn," I told him. So Ed filled Oliver and William in on the unauthorized activity going on at the Mint, the faked security footage, and the trucks we'd seen.

"I also spoke with K," Phil said. She'd warned that if the government continued to flood the market with dollars, they would eventually devalue to the point of being worthless. And not just because of the bailouts. There was also the debt. We'd soon be unable to pay it back. The Chinese would only buy so much, and printing dollars would be the only way. To avoid an economic collapse, the government could step in and exchange dollars for a new currency.

"You don't know this," Oliver said, shaking his head.

"Maybe we do. Just look at the coin Todd gave us." I handed it to him. When Oliver read *AMERO* out loud, the room grew still. His brow puckered, and he stared at the coin, and then repeatedly turned it over in his hand. He then handed it to William and we waited.

"Okay, what's the plan?" Oliver said, looking at Phil.

"William?" Phil asked.

William nodded. "Go ahead."

"We'll file a Qui tam action. Todd's agreed to be the whistleblower, and he'll be at our meeting with Pete on Sunday." Phil then explained that we'd also file a second lawsuit in Federal Court. The FCA's mandatory filing under seal and gag order with no judicial review violates the filer's first amendment right to speak.

"And you'll enjoy this Rachel. We'll be suing the US Attorney General since he heads the Department of Justice, and they're responsible for defending federal laws," Phil added.

"We could? That would be great! Teach him not to bribe me," I said with relish. The AG had offered Oliver, Phil, and RD judicial appointments to drop the dead lawyer case, but ignored me. I didn't know if this was how karma was supposed to work, but it felt good.

"Rachel, let it go!" everyone shouted.

"Thanks a lot," I muttered.

"Okay." Phil started pacing. "We give Pete all the info on Sunday, before the gag orders, and have him broadcast right after we file Monday."

"Would you consider giving Uncle Pete the copy? Imagine what the wrong people might do with the real key. If we could understand its markings before making it public..."

"I stashed it in a safe place. No one will find it," Ed said, and the guys agreed to consider it. Phil then told us he'd already spoken to Arthur.

"My brother-in-law thinks we're crazy, and was reluctant, until I reminded him we're family and threatened to sic Lynn on him," Phil joked. "He arranged for me to visit the grove with him tomorrow."

I was grateful Arthur was helping us, but suspected he was persuaded by whatever Phil had on him—why he owed Phil big time—and not familial ties. Then again, people go to crazy lengths for family, so who knows. Ed then told us he'd have all the equipment ready, and we called it a night.

Standing, I looked around the room at my fellow warriors and knew Master Sun Tzu would be proud.

CHAPTER 22

The next morning we drove to Phil's house. Ed stopped his jeep in the drive of the mansion and pushed the intercom adjacent to a nine-foot iron scrollwork fence encircling the property. The gates parted, and we drove inside and down into an underground garage. The four-story house was built into the hill.

Lynn greeted us, and we followed her upstairs to the main floor. Phil stood outside the family room and said Arthur was there. He also warned us about Arthur's new hairpiece and cautioned us not to laugh.

"He claims it's a hit with the ladies." Phil rolled his eyes. He then let us into the room.

I greeted Arthur with a hug. His overpowering cologne was almost as horrible as his badly dyed hairpiece. We exchanged pleasantries and sat on the sofa. Lynn showed John and Geoffrey into the room ten minutes later. Ed introduced Geoffrey to Phil and Arthur, and the young man shyly shook their hands. He then seemed to notice me and turned red. We'd met a handful of times, and Ed said I made him nervous. I had no idea why. Geoffrey waved and I walked over.

"Hello, there." I then told him I wanted to hear all about his girlfriend. His pale skin turned redder, and his shaggy hair fell in front of his eyes. How cute. I'd once labeled him the classic nerd, late twenties, skinny arms dangling from a loose and well-worn

T-shirt, and awkward. Not any longer. A hacking virtuoso with a sense of humor, there was more to him.

Ed and John fitted Phil and Arthur with concealed cameras and microphones and then went over the plan. The men were to stop shortly after driving inside the grove to stretch their legs giving us a few minutes to park and set up our equipment. A satellite dish for aerial coverage was rigged to the top of our "hippie" van, a vehicle in top-notch working order even though peeling paint, rust, dings, and scratches marred the late model's outer surface. The men would later take a "drunken" walk around the grove so we could see what was going on.

At 10:00 a.m. Arthur and Phil drove north on Highway 101 over the Golden Gate Bridge. Ed, John, Geoffrey, and I followed in the hippie van. Ninety minutes later we passed Arthur's Mercedes as it stopped at the entrance to Bohemian Grove. John parked our van at an encampment housing small campers and RVs nearly a quarter mile down the road. I stepped out to stretch my legs and was greeted by an odd assortment of people: hippies, transients, and good witches casting spells to counteract the black magic allegedly practiced at the grove. My mouth dropped open. Ed joined me and smiled at my reaction.

"Darlin', you ain't in the big city anymore," he said with a twang.

"That's for sure."

I looked around again, awed by the giant redwoods nestled among the deep-green foliage of the forest. The imposing trees had lived for centuries. Breathing deeply, I smelled the fresh air and moist greenery surrounding me. Not the pollution smells I was used to. After taking another deep cleansing breath, I worked the kinks from my shoulders and followed Ed back inside. There I watched Geoffrey's fingers fly across his keyboard, his eyes glued to the monitors in front of him. I heard him say, "Gotcha" and the darkened screens came alive. One showed an aerial view of the grove. Another followed the digital feed coming from the camera and microphone in the American flag pin attached to

Phil's golf shirt. A third monitor captured the view from the camera concealed in Arthur's toupee, a location I thought genius despite its dreadful look.

We soon watched as they drove up the road to the main lodge. Moments later they alighted and turned in a 360-degree circle to seemingly admire the scenery. We now had a visual of the compound. The men then went inside and joined several of Arthur's friends for cocktails. An hour later they set out on a nature walk as agreed.

"Breathe that fresh air," Phil said and drew a deep breath.

Arthur concurred and they set off at a slow pace away from the lodge, Phil carrying a bottle of scotch. We watched as they walked deep into the surrounding forest that was artistically sprinkled with ancient redwood trees. The men roved about, the video feed in the van showing everything they saw.

When they entered a clearing with a large lake bordered by an amphitheater composed of a wooden stage with rough-hewn seats, John said, "This must be where they do the Cremation of Care Ceremonies."

"Looks like it," Ed agreed, staring at the monitors.

"The what?" I asked.

Ed explained that every July the grove held a two-week celebration. During this time the super-rich, corporate chieftains, high government officials, and celebrity artists gathered for the annual ceremonies. What actually went on there remained a mystery. The theories ranged from occult rituals by men clad in hooded black robes offering human sacrifices to be burned alive, to just harmless theatrical fun.

Both sounded ridiculous, yet I knew Master Sun Tzu embraced confusion as a means of deceiving an audience from what was truly happening. So I nodded when Ed finished and returned to the monitor to watch my warriors slowly turn in a 360-degree circle again before heading back in the direction of the main lodge. Ten minutes later they ambled across a dirt road. Arthur stopped and motioned at the bottle. Phil signaled okay and opened the scotch. After taking what looked like a huge swig and spilling some on himself, he handed it to Arthur who did the same. The two men then set off once again.

Arthur had told us there were areas that were open to only a select few. Many of them were guarded by the grove's private security force. Tales of global leaders plotting the world's destiny and secret rituals passed down from generation to generation had reached Arthur, but he'd discounted them as the mad ravings of conspiracy nuts. Instead, he'd accepted that certain individuals required separate and secure quarters for their protection. Yet, after what Phil had shared, he was no longer so sure, and agreed to wander into a few private areas he knew of.

And so I watched Phil and Arthur meander through the trees. They were playing the little old men routine to the hilt, walking at a snail's pace with their postures stooped. The men continued moving through the foliage. At one point Arthur stopped to lean on a nearby tree, appearing to catch his breath. Phil joined him. Moments later I heard Phil say, "Carry on." Arthur and Phil started walking again, their pace even slower. The men had walked another fifty feet when an armed guard dressed in fatigues stepped into their path.

"You can't come in here."

Swaying, Arthur slurred, "Excuse me, young man, we're on our way to the lodge."

The guard stared at him. His nostrils flared, and his nose wrinkled with distaste as he noticed their scotch cologne and intoxicated demeanor. His stance softened.

"Gentlemen, you need to follow the dirt road on the right," he said pointing. "This area is unsafe."

"Really?" Phil questioned, hiccupping.

"Yes, sir," the guard said, then turned Arthur and gave him a light push toward the road he'd indicated.

"Thank you, good man," Arthur garbled, saluting.

Phil nodded and leaned closer, before hugging the man. The guard shoved Phil away, and I watched him lose his balance and fall to the ground. Phil looked stunned, and anger bubbled through me. How dare he, the bully!

"Phil, are you hurt?" I yelled at the monitor.

The guard must have had the same thought because he asked, "Are you injured, sir?"

Phil looked up, his brow furrowed as if dazed, and slowly shook his head. Thank goodness. The guard took Phil's arm and helped him up, Phil leaning all over him as he did. Once he stood, the guard moved Phil a foot away. Phil swayed and reached a hand out to steady himself. The guard took Phil's arm again and brought him over to Arthur, before walking both men to the road he'd indicated.

"Gentlemen, I'd suggest some coffee." He saluted, turned, and returned to his station.

I watched my warriors smile at each other. Phil made a covert thumbs-up signal, and Geoffrey started playing with another computer station. Seconds later we heard the guard tell someone that the old men were just a couple of drunks who'd lost their way. Another man laughed in response. We heard some rustling noises, and all was quiet again. The guard would hopefully never discover the pin receiver Phil had dropped on his clothing.

Twenty minutes later my warriors were back at the lodge. They left the grove shortly thereafter, and our van followed them back to Phil's house. Ed and John removed all the spy gear and we called it a day.

The following morning Geoffrey phoned while we were in the kitchen having breakfast. Ed pushed speakerphone and I heard the pin microphone recording was ready. Ed then called everyone and arranged a meeting at Oliver's that evening.

"Six, got it." I leaned in to kiss Ed's cheek. I put my dishes in the sink and went down the hall to my office. I had a lot of work to catch up on. At five I wandered into the kitchen and found Ed staring at his laptop screen. He looked up and then tapped his watch.

"I'll be ready." I grabbed a cookie and went to shower and

get dressed. I returned to find a grilled cheese sandwich waiting for me.

"So, was the recording useful?" I took a cheesy bite.

"Yes."

"And…"

"With the others," Ed said, and I sighed. Once I finished my sandwich, we left.

William was already seated in Oliver's den nursing a scotch when we walked in. Phil and Arthur arrived soon after.

"Oliver," Arthur greeted with a smile, and then a warm hug. "I was relieved to hear that you were doing well."

"Thanks Art." Oliver waited a beat before asking, "What's that on your head?"

"Oh, nothing, just a small enhancement."

"You're joking, right?" Oliver said.

Arthur seemed hurt, and I nudged Oliver.

"Sorry, Art," Oliver apologized. "Have a cookie," he offered, picking up a tin.

"Okay, now here's the audio tape from the mic Phil dropped on the guard. Listen carefully," Ed said, and the room grew quiet. I heard a few soft noises I couldn't place, and then the sounds of footfalls reached my ears.

"Any activity gentlemen?" a deep male voice asked.

"No, sir," another man said.

"Sir, two old drunks walked near the road this afternoon." That was the guard's voice.

"What?" asked the deep male voice.

"They were drunk, sir, and I sent them toward the lodge. They never saw the vault, sir."

Vault, what vault? Oh, my gosh!

"Are you sure?" deep voice said.

"Yes, sir, they were too far away," the guard confirmed.

"I want to know if anyone comes anywhere near here. Is that understood?"

"Yes, sir," the subordinates replied as one.

"There will be another shipment of supplies in a few days, and the location must be secure. Am I understood?"

"Yes, sir," they chorused once more.

I heard receding footsteps, and the quiet returned. Ed switched off the tape with a click.

"Wow!" I felt stunned. I looked around the room at everyone's shocked expressions, and repeated, "Wow!"

"You're not kidding, wow," Phil said. "A vault and a shipment."

"It makes sense if they're up to skullduggery," Arthur announced as he stood and inserted his right hand in the hip pocket of his black trousers.

"Skullduggery?"

"Yes Rachel, skullduggery. Unscrupulous behavior. The word is used in all the *Bond* movies."

How sweet, the guy thinks he's James Bond.

Ed then told us he was watching the Mint. One of his guys had rented a place off Buchanan Street a block away and was staking it out. He'd also have some men lined up for a possible reconnaissance to get into the vault, if needed.

"Ed, the guard had a gun," I said.

"Just preparations, babe. Pete will be here tomorrow. Let's see what happens."

My elation quickly changed to fear. Ed may have downplayed my dream, but I hadn't. I wanted him as far away from guns as possible.

•   •   •

Pete walked into Phil's living room with his two-man camera crew late Sunday afternoon.

"Uncle Pete," I cried out.

He winced.

I hugged him and inspected his freshly groomed brows. "You handsome old devil." He'd finally used the spa gift card I'd given him for his birthday.

Pete stepped back and noticed Todd. We introduced the two

men and let Todd fill him in on the Mint, the coin, and Joe's disappearance.

"It gets better." Phil told him about the false security footage, the trucks, and the grove. And then he showed him the coin.

"Unbelievable," Pete murmured, flipping it over. His crew seemed mesmerized.

"We'll never be able to prove what's been going on at the Mint with the fake security footage," Phil said, "but by making it all public we can get the media machine investigating."

We also wanted Dillingham to leave us alone, and if we no longer had the key and the microchip, hopefully he would.

"Okay, so what do you want?" Pete asked, and Phil told him about the two lawsuits, and how the gag orders that would result necessitated us sharing everything now. We gave him the original microchip, the images, and the duplicate key to televise, and Pete took lots of footage of the coin. We needed to keep it for Todd's lawsuit.

"Can you get station time in the morning?" Phil asked, and Pete assured us it wouldn't be a problem.

"Terrific! Now we booked you a suite at the Palace Hotel under the name Wiley Coyote. Only the best for you, Uncle Pete." Grand and luxurious, the historic hotel had survived the legendary 1906 earthquake and was famous for its celebrity clientele. We'd also arranged two bodyguards for him and his crew. Uncle Pete looked suspiciously at me, and I smiled. Keeping him uneasy was just as much fun as tormenting him.

Todd then called work to say he would be out sick for a few days. He was actually going to stay at Phil's. It was like a fortress, and he'd be safe. Ed went with Todd to pack a bag, and John accompanied Pete to the Palace. While they were gone, Phil and I went over the documents we'd prepared this morning, and called it a day when they returned.

Ed seemed unusually quiet on the drive to his house. We went to bed early, and as I was falling asleep, he whispered, "We stick together until we know it's safe."

"Sure, Ed," I said, now wide awake.

CHAPTER 23

It was eight o'clock on Monday morning, and I sat in Phil's enormous chef's kitchen sipping my fourth cup of coffee. An associate at Phil's law firm had flown cross-country to file our Qui tam lawsuit with the Washington D.C. Federal Court, and we were waiting to hear from him.

"Can we go now?" I jumped out of my seat.

"Rachel, sit down!" Once I sat, Phil continued. "You have got to learn to contain yourself. If you plan to move from ingénue to first chair, poise and control are crucial." He then took my coffee cup from me and put it in the sink. "And no more coffee for you."

"Yes, Phil," I said, recalling Master Sun Tzu instructed poise as well. I might get wound up, but I didn't have to show it. So I sat quietly, armed in my lucky white shirt and navy suit. Thirty minutes later, the phone rang.

"Great, thanks, Jim," Phil said, and hung up. "He just filed it, let's go."

Ed and John accompanied us into the limousine parked in Phil's underground garage and we left. Turning, I watched the metal gates close behind us as we drove away.

We arrived at the Federal Courthouse in fifteen minutes. My posse and I crossed the battle lines and entered the courthouse shortly after nine. Ed wheeled the box containing our motions and lawsuit. We walked up to the clerk's desk, and John hefted the box onto the counter.

"We have an expedited hearing request, and the complaint is for declaratory relief and an injunction," Phil said.

The clerk nodded and took the proffered documents. "Requests go to the presiding judge in Department 15. Wait outside his chambers."

"Thank you," Phil said, and we left.

A moment later we stood outside the presiding judge's closed door. To wait—that foul four-letter expletive once again. Amped up on coffee and anxious, I took a seat and tried to remain calm. I stared at Phil frenetically pacing. His mad race up and down the hall had me feeling even more nervous.

"Could you stop? It's making me crazy."

Phil looked at me. "No." He marched on.

We waited outside the presiding judge's chambers for almost an hour. When the PJ's clerk finally opened the door and ushered us inside the waiting area, my nerves felt shot. The judge looked up from his desk and waved us into his back chambers. He then stared at Phil, and said, "I thought you retired."

"I did, but this case came to my attention, Your Honor," Phil said.

"I see. I'm concerned about standing. You filed as Plaintiff John Doe."

"And asked for an expedited hearing to seal the party's true name in order to preserve our client's anonymity," Phil said.

"Our client filed a Qui tam action," I added.

"So you thought you'd get around the gag order by having an anonymous John Doe bring this lawsuit without disclosing the contents of the Qui tam action, who filed it, and when. Is that the gist of it?" the judge said as his clerk knocked and walked in.

"I'm sorry, Your Honor, but you need to see this," the judge's clerk said. He then turned on the TV in the corner, and we watched Uncle Pete's live broadcast featuring close-ups of the house key, microchip, and unscrambled images, and a story on how a murdered John Bush had sent it to him fearing his demise, a small fib to keep us out of the story. He then showed footage of the AMERO coin and aired his account of the funny business going on at the San Francisco Mint, and how Joe Collins, a Federal officer had vanished. We knew it would be on YouTube and all over the Internet before we left the courthouse.

"Is this what you're involved in?" The judge glared at us.

His anger was understandable. Ed's background check on Judge Franklin revealed he was being vetted for a Federal Appellate Court appointment, meaning he wouldn't want to do anything to rock the boat. Deciding against the Justice Department could be political suicide, and he knew it.

"Your Honor," Phil started, but the judge cut him off. "I don't want to know. Here's your order." He handed the signed document to Phil.

"Thank you, Your Honor," Phil and I said in unison, and left to the judge complaining, "Of all the courtrooms, in all the courthouses, in all the world..."

Armed with a signed order, we filed the remaining documents with the court clerk and arranged to have the relevant parties served. We then headed to Oliver's. He wasn't happy about having to sit on the sidelines but understood it was only for a little while longer. I was therefore surprised when he greeted us at the elevator with champagne.

"It's all over the Internet," he said grinning. "Time to celebrate."

• • •

At seven the next morning the doorman phoned to tell me there were several gentlemen who wished to speak with me. I had him hold while I turned on the TV and switched to the security display of my condo's lobby. The screen showed two men dressed in dark conservative suits and who had buzz-style haircuts. They looked like government types, but I couldn't rule out Dillingham's thugs.

My warriors suspected the government might try some muscle. They never played nicely when caught doing things they shouldn't. Say for example, the unauthorized use of the Mint.

And so we'd already decided the initial meeting would be on our turf where we could film the discussion. One of Ed's team had installed hidden cameras in my law firm's conference room last night. Secretly taping them wasn't exactly legal, so we'd placed a sign in the lobby informing visitors that our premises were secured by close-circuit TV. Cameras were clearly visible in the lobby and hallways. The fact they couldn't see the ones in the conference room was irrelevant. Notice was notice.

"Ask them if they have a warrant," I instructed the doorman. The taller one scowled, and shook his head.

"Tell them I will meet with them at my office at noon, and that it's inappropriate for them to come to my home."

I could see their disbelief followed by anger as the doorman conveyed my message. The taller one turned to the security camera and glared, before nodding and motioning to the other. They both slipped on their mirrored sunglasses and left. I then moved to the window and watched them get into a large black four-door sedan double parked in front of my building. Ed was already there covertly taking pictures.

A moment later the telephone rang. It was Phil calling to warn us that several goons had appeared outside his security fence asking for admittance to his home. They didn't have a warrant and were directed to Acker and Kendall's law office at noon. Thank goodness for locked gates and secure buildings.

Thirty minutes later Uncle Pete phoned in. We knew it would take the goons a little longer to locate him. Uncle Pete let us know he was fine. They'd found him in the Pied Piper Bar, the Palace's lounge which housed the famous Maxfield Parrish mural. The Pied Piper of Hamlin led you anywhere he wished, and the laughing child's eyes in the painting followed you wherever you went in the room. It seemed a fitting place to meet the goons. Uncle Pete sat in a back booth with William, two bodyguards, and a cameraman ready to film. After acknowledging their lack of a warrant, they'd been directed to our office at noon. Uncle Pete said they'd been furious and left in a huff.

"Silly goons. Emotion had no place in battle," I said, quoting Master Sun Tzu.

• • •

Two goons showed up at noon. We let them wait for twenty minutes before William's assistant showed the men to the conference room. Phil, William, Uncle Pete, and I stood when they entered, and William asked to see their identification. Each opened a leather billfold showing a metal badge and laminated photo ID from the Department of Justice. I asked for a closer look, and they reluctantly handed them over. I held them up for the cameras to record, and then "accidentally" dropped them. Although the identifications seemed real to me, we needed to confirm these men were from the government and not Dillingham's thugs. So as soon as the IDs hit the ground, I bent to recover them and slipped the FBI issued surveillance pin John had given me into a goon's pant cuff. Standing, I returned the IDs.

"So, how can we assist you, gentlemen?" Phil asked once everyone was seated.

The tall one from this morning stared at Uncle Pete. "We're here to talk about Mr. Simpson's broadcast yesterday." I'd already forgotten his name, and labeled him Tall Goon.

"Whatever do you mean?" Phil inquired.

Tall Goon's flat eyes blinked at Phil's question. I suspect a six-foot-three muscular G-man with a gun and a badge was imposing to most. He was not used to being questioned. Well, my warriors were not most, they were the best. I'd side with a scrappy five-foot-eight Phil any day. And so I sat back and watched Phil pull the tiger's tail, certain Master Sun Tzu would have found a kindred spirit.

"We are here to investigate when and how Mr. Simpson acquired the information for his newscast about the AMERO coin yesterday morning," Tall Goon continued.

"Pete, when did you acquire the information for your newscast on the coin?" Phil inquired.

"Sunday," Uncle Pete said, and I watched Tall Goon blink. Not what he wanted to hear. Providing information to the media before a Qui tam action's filed doesn't violate anything.

"And who did you get your information from?" Tall Goon asked.

Phil nodded and Uncle Pete said, "Sorry, but I won't reveal my source."

A third blink, and a muscle clenched in Tall Goon's jaw. "Mr. Simpson, we can arrest you for interference with an ongoing investigation."

"Go right ahead, but I'm certain the resulting media will direct a great deal more attention exactly where you don't want it." *Bravo, Uncle Pete!*

Another blink. Tall Goon reached inside his suit jacket and pulled out a subpoena, and dropped it on the table. "You have been served, Mr. Simpson," he said, and stood. His partner joined him and they exited the room. William followed to make sure they left. I picked up the subpoena and smiled. It ordered Uncle Pete to turn everything he had on the AMERO over to the Department of Justice. They were doing exactly what we wanted.

Master Sun Tzu would be proud.

•   •   •

Ed's team swept our offices—and us—shortly after the goons left. Nothing was found. The goons were not as vigilant. We confirmed they were DOJ and not Dillingham's thugs before disconnecting the listening device an hour later.

At three, Uncle Pete stood outside the clerk's office in the Federal Building, while his camera crew filmed him holding the key, microchip, and images. He reported he was depositing the lot with the clerk of the Federal Court. Phil and I stood next to him. I then held up the AMERO coin, and Phil said we were placing it with the court for safekeeping. Uncle Pete added his concerns about Officer Joe Collins's continued absence and the murder of John Bush, and we walked inside. Ed, John, and two burly bodyguards followed. Uncle Pete's camera crew recorded the exchange with the clerk, and we exited the building with receipts for our deposits shortly thereafter.

Uncle Pete's report aired repeatedly on the news and went viral online. Now everyone knew everything we had was now in the hands of the Feds. Dillingham no longer had any reason to go after us, and hopefully we were all safe.

Hopefully.

CHAPTER 24

Ed and I had just returned home when John phoned. We needed to get over to Roy's apartment by the Mint immediately. On the drive over Ed told me Roy was his guy who'd been staking out the Mint.

"What's going on?" Ed asked as soon as Roy's front door closed behind us.

"Roy hasn't checked in or answered his phone." John paused. "And I found blood."

"Blood?" I said, worried.

John motioned for us to follow as he walked toward the bathroom. Traces of dried blood were visible on the green tile floor. Someone had done a very sloppy job of wiping up. Ed stiffened and then rotated his shoulders in an obvious effort to relax.

"Was he working on anything else?" Ed asked.

"Who knows? It could be unrelated, and there's no sign of a break-in, but he's always been reliable. It's not like him not to check in. And the blood…"

Ed nodded. "Let's go." He unlocked the door and checked the hallway before we walked out. While John locked the deadbolt, I noticed someone peering at us from a few doors down. Moving closer, I knocked and asked if we could speak. After a long pause, the door opened wider, and I saw the metal security chain and a bespectacled senior citizen.

"Hello there. We're friends of your neighbor," I said, pointing at Roy's front door. "We were supposed to get together, and he's not here. Did you happen to see him leave?"

"Yes."

"Oh, when was that?"

"He went for a run at…" He shut the door. I looked over at the men and shrugged. A moment later the door opened, and he said, "11:53 p.m."

"He hasn't been back since?"

A pause and then he shut the door again. Seconds passed before he reopened it to say, "At 5:41 a.m., and he left at 5:57 a.m. with two men."

"Two men?"

"One on each side. They were helping him downstairs."

"I see." Not wanting to frighten him I tried to look casual as I asked, "I don't suppose you noticed where they went?"

"To a blue car."

"A blue car. Hmmm, do you know what kind of car?"

"No."

"Oh."

"But I have the license plate number if you want it."

What? She needed to stay calm. "That would be wonderful."

The door closed again. When Roy's nosy neighbor finally reopened the door, I noticed him holding a small spiral. "Neighborhood watch," he said when he spotted where I was looking.

"An important job. Could I possibly see your notebook?"

He looked me up and down a bit before agreeing. He closed the door, and I could hear him unfastening the chain. I remained where I was, motioning to the men to stay back so they wouldn't spook him. The door opened, and the watchful senior held a little blue notebook in his hands. I moved closer and he opened it. Seconds later he pointed at a page.

"This is it, California license plate number 5CZC861 at 5:57 a.m."

I wrote it down and thanked him. He smiled, and I slipped

him my business card, requesting he phone if Roy returned, or anything odd occurred.

"Odd?"

I stopped and turned back toward him. "Yes, odd."

"Lots of odd things going on over there," he said, waving in the direction of the Mint. "Trucks going in and out of there at all hours of the night."

"Really," I said, now fascinated.

"Yes, see." He tapped a page. "Thirteen times in the last month. Don't know what they're doing, but it is odd."

"Mr…"

"Callahan…Uh, Percy."

"Percy, I'm Rachel. I'm a lawyer. And really worried about my friend. Would it be okay if I copied a few pages from your notebook?" I held up my phone.

"I don't know…"

"It will only take a few minutes."

"Well, Harriet hasn't had her dinner." Percy stepped back and closed the door once again. When he opened it, he was holding a large furry orange cat in his arms. "She's beautiful," I told him.

"You know I called the police, but they didn't believe me."

"Well, I believe you."

Percy smiled. He then handed me the book and anxiously watched as I copied the entire contents.

Walking downstairs the men found splattered blood on the worn carpet and along the lobby's tile floor. Ed's jaw clenched and John's hands balled into fists as we left the building.

"Ed, do you think Lynn might have a friend for Percy?" I asked on the drive home.

"What is it with you and matchmaking?"

"I can't help it. I'm in love so I want the whole world to be happy and in love too."

"Do you need to be the one to bring it about?"

"Well, no, but he's lonely. Can't we help him?"

Ed just sighed and kept driving.

• • •

I put on a pot of coffee as soon as we reached Ed's place. John arrived minutes later and told us he'd called Geoffrey about the license plate. He'd asked him to also look at satellite and video footage around the Mint between eleven last night and seven this morning. John then joined us at the kitchen table, reviewing Percy's book. The man didn't sleep. Around-the-clock entries detailed the comings and goings of Percy's neighbors and any street activity for the last few months.

"I think Roy found something. He usually went out for around twenty minutes. The day of the last truck departure, Roy was gone almost eight hours," Ed said. Standing, he started to pace. "Okay, we need to assume that Roy might have given us up. We also need to assume he might be dead."

Dead? We were supposed to be safe now.

Ed and John phoned my warriors' security details to alert them. They were on lockdown and told not to leave their homes. Once that was done, Ed said it was time to figure out the key's meaning. He phoned someone, and arranged to meet with him late tomorrow afternoon. A muscle in Ed's jaw kept clenching. I reached over and gently touched his cheek, before covering his hand and assuring him everything would be okay.

"We're the good guys," I added with a smile.

Ed grimaced.

It would have to do.

• • •

Geoffrey was able to hack into the security software at the Mint perimeter and get footage of two men following Roy back to his apartment. With their heads down and the poor lighting, we were unable to identify them, yet they seemed familiar. Ed thought they might be the guys who'd broken into my apartment. Geoffrey also hacked into various motor vehicle surveillance cameras and watched the blue car drive north over the Golden Gate, before it disappeared.

We returned to Roy's apartment the following morning. John was certain there was a clue somewhere. Not knowing what to do, I looked under the bed and saw a number of boxes. Kneeling, I pulled everything out and found a surprise.

"Hey, look guys, he has a *Star Wars* droid…" No response. "And there are four boxes."

That got their attention. Unfortunately, they didn't find anything of value. The boxes only stored extra clothes. Twenty minutes later, they stopped searching.

"What about the droid? We can't leave him here."

"Rachel, it's just a toy," John said.

"He's coming with us." Ed picked up the robot.

"Whatever, let's go," John said, walking to the front door.

CHAPTER 25

We drove past Fisherman's Wharf and Pier 39, and merged onto the Embarcadero heading east toward AT&T Park, home of the San Francisco Giants. We were meeting Ed's guy, a professor of semiology, at his office near the ballpark. I felt that uncomfortable pressure between my shoulder blades as we neared, and tried not to panic.

"We're being followed," Ed said a block from the stadium. "Blue sedan, three cars back." He parked in a nearby lot, handed me the parking stub, and grabbed his phone. "John, we're at AT&T Park. We're being followed. If I can't lose them inside, we'll meet you at Pier 39 by the sea lions." I took a pen from the glove compartment and jotted our location on the ticket, then shoved them both in my hip pocket. Looking up, I saw Ed at my door. He took my hand, and we headed for the ballpark.

We stopped at a traffic light, and Ed glanced around. It turned green, and we moved through the crowds toward the gigantic Willie Mays statue designating the park's southeast entrance. There Ed purchased two tickets from a scalper, and we walked inside. The heavenly aroma of garlic fries permeated the air. I gripped Ed's hand as we navigated hordes of fans, the heaviness between my shoulders now painful. Suddenly Ed stiffened.

"What?"

"They're right behind us, move!"

I quickened my step and followed him, terrified. And then we ducked behind a large rowdy group of men waiting on the long line for beer, and stopped. My body shook with fear.

"Now!" Ed tugged on my hand. We raced back the way we'd come, and then turned north, passing through the crowds to exit out the northeast corner. We continued walking. Ed abruptly turned and stopped to look about, before pulling me east toward McCovey Cove. The cove had a public dock and provided access to the bay bordering the ballpark.

Seconds later we entered a shop called The Scull. Life vests, slickers, and fishing nets adorned the walls. A young man stood behind the counter and looked at Ed. "Can I help you?"

"We'd like to rent a double kayak for the game."

"Above water?"

At Ed's nod he quoted the rates and had Ed fill out some paperwork. I'd watched aquatic fans hoping to catch a ball on television, but it was not something I had ever wanted to do with the bay's freezing winds and murky green icy water. Yet I was more afraid of whoever was following us, and didn't hesitate to put on the weather gear Ed handed me. Ed then carried a kayak to the cove's public dock, and I stepped inside. Chilled, my teeth started chattering. Ed got in behind me, and we paddled out of the cove into the bay, before turning west toward Pier 39.

"Are they still following us?" I asked twenty minutes later. The feeling between my shoulder blades had subsided.

"I don't think so. Let's go a little farther."

Nodding, I ignored my aching shoulders and frostbitten hands, and continued to watch the horizon and paddle. When I saw something bob above the water's surface, I screamed.

"What?" Ed snapped.

"On the right." My heart thundered.

"It's just an otter, Rachel. Now veer toward the shore. I'm more concerned with two-legged animals right now."

The panic ebbed, and I paddled inland as directed. In no time we were pulling abreast of a deserted pier and tethering the kayak to a metal ladder built into one of the dock's long wooden pylons.

Ed climbed out, crossed the paddles inside the kayak, and then assisted me onto the wharf. After stowing the remaining gear, we made our way to the street. We were only a half mile west of the stadium and back at the Embarcadero in front of Pier 3.

Ed cautiously glanced about, and then hailed a taxi. "Pier 39," he instructed and closed the car door.

We arrived at the Pier's main entrance moments later. Ed looked around. He took my hand, and we headed around the side and toward the sea lions. The area appeared empty except for a lone man leaning against the rail. Ed pulled me closer, and our steps slowed. The man pushed away from the rail and straightened. He turned, and the air swooshed from my lungs as I recognized John. Relieved, I waved. As soon as we reached him, Ed let go of my hand, and I moved aside.

"What's going on?" John stepped closer.

And then I heard something whiz past me followed by a thump. When it happened again, I looked up to tell Ed and froze. In slow motion I watched Ed's body spin as blood splattered from his head before he slumped to the ground. John grabbed him and pulled him toward the rail, then dragged him over the recessed side. I knew I was screaming, yet somewhere my mind registered John's yell to get down, but it was too late. A foul-smelling cloth clamped over my nose and mouth, and I couldn't breathe.

Consciousness slipped away.

Ed covered in blood, my last thought.

CHAPTER 26

I awoke to my head throbbing. Pain stabbed at my temples and spasms assaulted my body. I felt horrible. And then I remembered what happened and bellowed like a wounded animal. Ed, my Ed. And blood. Dripping from his head as he fell into the water. Bile rose in my throat, and I huddled in a fetal position with my eyes clenched shut.

"Where is it?" Old D demanded.

My eyes burned as I opened them and looked up. The small windowless room was empty except for Old D, his son, and two muscular armed men dressed in green military fatigues standing in front of a heavy-looking metal door.

"Where is what?" My tongue felt thick, and it was hard to speak. My breathing grew labored. Gasping, I sat up. I then used the wall to help me stand and faced Old D.

"Miss Ballentine, you are quite aware of what I mean. Where is the key?"

"Key?" I took a deep breath to quell the rising nausea. "Where am I?"

"Do not anger me further."

"What?" The room started to spin. Swaying, I put my hand out to steady myself. My eyes closed and I slowly reopened them.

"Mr. Brogan is dead. You are next. Now, where is the key?" Old D said.

My legs shook and buckled, and I collapsed on the dirt floor.

Hands roughly grabbed me and dragged me upright. A guard then shoved me. Falling backwards, I smacked my head against the cement wall with a loud whack that reverberated through my skull.

"Ohhhh," I moaned.

"This act will do you no good. The key?" When I remained silent he added, "So be it. Do with her as you wish."

Young D ran his hand down my arm and my stomach turned. The nausea grew worse, and I tasted bile. Gagging, I threw up on his shirt, my body wracking with spasms.

"Ugggg, you bitch!" Young D cried out, backhanding me across the face. My ears rang, and I tasted blood as I collapsed to the floor once again.

"Leave her," Old D instructed.

A moment later I heard them walk away. I remained on the dirt floor. Its coldness helped calm some of the nausea, but couldn't relieve the assault on my mind. Pictures of Ed nervously revealing he was courting me, sharing our first kiss, and bent on one knee proposing, lashed out at me. Our first New Year's, his face as he unwrapped the *Star Wars* droid, and the sweet morning notes he left on my pillow, crashed around me. The tears freely flowed. The pain felt unbearable.

Time passed as I lay huddled on the floor. How long I had no idea. At some point I fell asleep. When I woke, my head felt better, and the nausea had subsided. *Okay, think Rachel.* Thoughts of Ed appeared, and a fresh wave of pain engulfed me. *Stop it!* I wiped the tears from my face.

Sitting up, I emptied my pockets. The parking stub, a pen, thirty dollars, and a piece of gum. Not much. I opened the wrapper and slowly chewed, and then winced. I gingerly touched alongside my jaw where Young D hit me, and flinched. *Ignore it!* And then a sensation of warmth surrounded me as I heard *the pen.* I picked it up, and turned the pen over several times in my hands. When I clicked the tip a ballpoint appeared, and retracted when I clicked it again. I then unscrewed the middle.

"What?" I said, touching a concealed USB connector. I restored the pen and looked at it more closely. This time I noticed a recession by the clip and the side. *Audio and video?* I wondered, knowing Ed's penchant for spy gadgets. Okay, assuming it was, how does this help? I could catch Dillingham on tape and somehow use it against him. Of course, if I didn't get out of here… No! I was getting out, and Ed was fine.

Suddenly I heard footsteps outside, followed by the heavy metal door unlocking. I shoved the money and stub in my pants. I then slipped the pen in my shirt pocket, clicking the end just as Old D and his son walked in with their armed escort.

"I have come back one last time. Where is the key?" Old D demanded.

"We gave it to the Feds," I said, staring at him. "And why would you want it? The computer chip was removed."

"Your choice," he said with a shrug.

"You're going to kill me anyway."

"Yes, but the choice of how is yours. A bullet is swift. Being burned alive I'm told is not an easy death." The corners of his mouth lifted in a sneer and black wrapped around him.

"Why do you want the key?" I said, facing him.

"I will not discuss this with you. For the last time, where is the key?"

The room grew still.

"Fine, tie her hands," Old D ordered, his tone nasty.

"And gag her," Young D instructed.

The guards yanked my hands together and tied them, but I felt numb. My Ed. He looked all hard and tough with his abundance of muscles, but he was a softy inside. Images of us returned to attack my mind. *Stop it!* I told myself as a rag was stuffed in my mouth. I gagged.

"Enough now get in," Young D said, as a guard wheeled in a long narrow wooden box.

"I did say burn," Old D added.

Knowing it would be useless to fight, I stepped up to stand

inside the box. Young D shoved me, and I fell with a hard thump.

"Now, now, son," Old D said, as the armed men grabbed my legs and bound my ankles with thick rope. He then ordered me to lie down.

"One last chance. The key? A bullet to the head will be easier."

My skin crawled at Old D's menacing look, but I remained quiet.

"So be it." Old D motioned to the guards, who lifted and placed a wooden lid over me. I felt them hammering it shut seconds later.

Angels, my mind screamed as tremors shook my body, and terror took hold. Warmth wrapped around me, and I heard *you are not alone*. The shakes slowly abated.

I remained inside the box for what seemed like hours. My breathing shallow at first, deepened when I noticed small shadows of light piercing the lid. Air holes—I wouldn't suffocate. Unwilling to give up, I tried to loosen the knots at my wrists. It was useless. I then attempted to bang my feet against the lid to no avail. I couldn't scream with the gag. All I could do was lie there and try to control the rising fear.

Listening carefully, I thought I heard moans.

Was I imagining them?

CHAPTER 27

I heard the door open and the sound of footsteps, and then felt the box being lifted and moved. The earlier shadows lightened, and I knew I was now outside. Moments later, I was put down. Something smelled familiar. Clean air and moist earth. And then I heard water sloshing about and realized where I was. My terror returned. Oliver, I silently screamed and sent a picture.

You are not alone I heard again, but this time the fear would not ebb. I was a prisoner to my watery grave. Bound inside, I lay there watching the shadows move while silently speaking to Oliver, and sending pictures. Eventually I dozed off again, abruptly waking to the sounds of a commotion.

They are here drifted in the air. The box jerked upward and my head hit the top with a loud thump. Seconds later I felt the lid being pried off. Fresh air teased my senses as the top was ripped away. When I saw Ed and John kneeling beside me, my heart raced and my muffled cries rang out.

"Quiet," Ed ordered, before lifting me from the wooden coffin and cradling me in his arms. His head was bandaged, and he looked exhausted. Yet he was solid and alive, and that's all that mattered. Tears fell unheeded.

"Time," John reminded.

Ed nodded and kissed the top of my head, then gently lay me down on the ground. He pulled a knife from an ankle sheath and cut the ropes at my hands and feet. He left the gag.

"This will hurt," Ed whispered and started massaging my legs, and then my arms. They'd cramped being tied in the box, and I wanted to scream. I didn't, biting my lip and remaining silent until the circulation returned. Once it had, Ed helped me stand. He then removed the gag and wiped the tears from my cheeks.

"I love you," I hoarsely whispered and took his hand.

We moved toward the forest's perimeter, where a handsome bearded man lay on the ground alongside another narrow wooden box. Blood matted a thick cloth wrapped around his right thigh, and he had numerous bruises.

John was kneeling behind him. "Roy, can you walk?"

"I don't think so. It's only a superficial wound, but..." He winced.

I heard a rustling noise and looked up. "No," I moaned.

"We thought it would be you," Old D said. His son stood next to him pointing a gun at us. John rose slowly while Roy turned on his left side to face our assailants. Ed moved in front of me.

"Very chivalrous, Mr. Brogan," Old D said with a sneer. "It appears we needed two bullets to exterminate you." He was breathing hard.

"Let her go. You have us," Ed said.

"Let her go? I don't think so," Old D responded with a laugh, then coughed. From the corner of my eye, I noticed John move closer to Roy. Lying on the ground, Roy's right arm draped behind him near John's feet. Did John have an ankle sheath like Ed?

"I want the key," Old D said.

I moved forward and waved my hands about hoping to distract Old D and his son. "Why do you want the key so bad? The contents of the microchip are already public."

"I want the key. Now!"

"Could it be the alpha tau chi omega?" I asked.

Old D grew eerily still. He then motioned toward his son. "So be it. Shatter his knee cap," he instructed, pointing at Ed.

Horrified, I moved closer. "What's the big deal," I said with disgust.

"Big deal. Big deal?" he repeated, his voice rising with anger. "That key holds the answer to understanding everything."

"That one key?"

"You stupid girl! You haven't a clue. There are thirteen keys. And they unlock everything. Unlimited knowledge to understand everything—control everything!" Old D yelled, his breathing labored.

Suddenly a shiny object flashed by me, and I saw the handle of a knife protruding from Young D's neck. He made a gurgling sound, and blood dripped down the front of his shirt. Old D turned toward his son, and let out an agonized shriek as he watched Young D crumple to the ground. He then clutched his chest, and fell to the floor. Ed grabbed the gun while John checked Young D's neck for a pulse. John shook his head and turned Old D over. I ran closer and saw Old D's unblinking upward stare.

"Ed, what do you want to do about the bodies?" John asked.

"I don't trust the cops. A cremation seems fitting," Roy answered.

"They knew the key was a copy. I'm with Roy," John said.

Ed hesitated, and then nodded. He told me to stay put, and handed the gun to Roy. I watched Ed and John hoist both bodies into the nearby wood box and set the makeshift coffin inside a large canoe parked by the water's edge. They found a nearby shack with gasoline and poured it over the improvised casket. The two shoved the canoe into the lake, and John threw a lit torch onto it. The explosion was deafening. I stared transfixed as the enormous flames engulfed the craft.

And then the wind shifted, and I looked at the dense foliage. Jet-black and crimson-red hues draped the nearby trees. Someone was out there, someone evil. Roy lay on the ground by my feet, and I felt him tense. He turned the gun toward the trees and told me to stay behind him. I saw the outline of two men in fatigues just as the strident sound of approaching sirens reached my ears. The men stopped moving. Seconds later the black-and-red shadows retreated back through the trees, and I relaxed.

When Ed and John returned, they helped Roy stand and assisted him toward the woods. As we moved through the forest, I noticed several men dressed in fatigues littering the ground. Gagged, with their arms and legs secured behind them, they were powerless.

"Shame on you!" I knelt and wagged my index finger in front of the face of the guard who'd shoved me. He growled in response.

"Rachel, come on," Ed ordered, and we headed toward the main lodge. Two of Ed's team joined us along the way, and I suspected they were responsible for the trussed-up men. Still shaky, I focused on moving as fast as I could and keeping up. The closer we got to the lodge, the more people I heard.

"Hide!" Ed said, and we blended back into the foliage as several firefighters ran past us. One shouted, "The lake," without stopping and raced on.

We reached the lodge, and I saw the Monte Rio Fire Department trucks and numerous volunteers. Fire in these parts could be treacherous. Relief coursed through me when I spotted our hippie van sitting at the perimeter of the parking lot. Ed signaled, and the driver moved the van closer. The men helped Roy and me inside, and closed the doors behind us. With all the commotion, no one appeared to notice us.

One of the men who'd joined us on the way back to the lodge, Gabe, was a trained medic. He immediately started attending to Roy's leg while John moved into the driver's seat, and drove us from the scene. I'd been shocked to see Oliver seated inside when I'd entered. I later learned he'd refused to stay behind, and had been left in charge of the van with Geoffrey. He placed a blanket around my shoulders and looked me over once I sat.

"I'm fine, Oliver."

"Are you sure?"

"Yes." I hugged him, knowing it would all catch up to me later.

"Good." Oliver picked up a thermos, poured me a cup of hot cocoa, and handed me a cookie. "Energy food," he told me.

I nodded, then sipped the warm beverage, my attention on Ed seated in front of me. He had closed his eyes, and he looked exhausted. Leaning forward, I put my hand on his shoulder. Ed placed his hand on mine.

No one spoke until Gabe said, "The bullet went straight through, he should be fine," a short time later. Roy lay in the back under several blankets and hooked to an IV bag. Gabe then moved next to Ed.

"Killer headache, I bet." He checked Ed's wound. Once he proclaimed, "You'll live," I relaxed.

"So, who needs a cookie?" Oliver asked.

Unable to help it, I laughed.

• • •

We drove back to the city and straight to the nearest hospital's emergency room. Roy was taken by stretcher inside. The next stop was my building. Ed and I got off the elevator on my floor, and John escorted Oliver upstairs. As soon as we were inside my apartment, Ed insisted on slowly undressing me. He wanted to personally make sure I was uninjured despite my assurances I only had a few scrapes.

On the ride home he'd explained that he placed a tracker in the earrings he gave me in case he "lost me." I'd completely forgotten to question him about them with all that had been happening. The signal had allowed Geoffrey to trail me via satellite. The men followed as soon as Ed had a few stitches sewn into his head and released himself from the hospital against doctor's orders.

Ed had also handed me Oliver's drawings—pictures of an eight-sided structure on a hill with lines drawn outward from the octagon's points. One line was pronounced and extended northwest to an area designated "GROVE" and an oblong shape marked with an X. The picture I'd sent Oliver. When I turned to Oliver, my brows shot up.

"We're on the same radio frequency, kiddo," he said.

Sighing, I looked at my dirty clothes balled on the bathroom floor, and noticed Ed's pen. Reaching down, I clicked the end, put it on the ledge of the sink, and leaned back into Ed's embrace. He'd insisted I needed a warm bath. He also declared that we needed to be more environmentally prudent and conserve water. Bathing together was an effective way.

"Ed, your pen." I motioned toward the sink.

"Hmmm, my pen?"

"Yeah, the one from your glove compartment. My angels told me about it."

"Your angels," he murmured, and then went still.

"Ed?"

"Is this the smoking pen?"

"Possibly."

CHAPTER 28

The following morning, Geoffrey came by, and we watched the pen's USB footage. It was difficult. I felt myself reliving the terror of being bound and nailed in the wood box all over again. Geoffrey ended the recording just after I was placed in the coffin and said it would appear untampered. When he started to explain why, I excused myself. I had enough stuff floating around in my head.

Uncle Pete broadcast the tape that evening, and we turned it over to the police the next day. I was a kidnap victim, held hostage at gunpoint because Dillingham mistakenly believed I had the key and microchip. At least that was our story, and both federal and state agencies were investigating. They told me an all points bulletin had been put out over the airwaves for the Dillinghams in connection with my kidnapping. Good luck finding them. Instead, I took comfort knowing the universe's scales of justice were pure and true, and they would get theirs, wherever their blackened and charred souls were residing.

So three days after my rescue, Ed and I sat in my sunny yellow kitchen perusing several newspapers. "Babe, listen to this," Ed said, reading a piece captioned "Burned Alive." It reported how a homeless man was set afire at Bohemian Grove, and his remains were so charred that even dental records couldn't be used for identification. It also noted how the Dillinghams had fled the grove and were last spotted in Sao Paulo. John had leaked stories of the Dillinghams's appearance in Brazil to further flame the fires, and I knew Master Sun Tzu would approve. He taught warriors to be magicians—misdirection a mighty weapon.

When Ed looked up from the newspaper, I reminded him that we still had the hidden key.

"Rachel, let's put it on the back burner for now. No one knows about it."

I thought of the black and red colors I'd seen near the lake, and knew this was not the end of it. "I don't know."

"You won't let it go, will you?"

"I can't."

Ed sighed. "Fine, if you won't drop it, how about we give the case to John to investigate?"

Looking at Ed's bandaged head, I agreed.

• • •

We went to visit Roy in the hospital that afternoon.

"Knock, knock," I said as we walked into his room.

"We brought you someone," Ed added and held up the *Star Wars* droid.

"You found my little friend." Roy smiled. Ed placed the robot in Roy's outstretched hands. "So, did you find it?" Roy asked.

"Find what?" Ed said.

"You didn't..." Roy trailed off looking at our puzzled expressions. "You're going to love this." He motioned for us to watch. Roy then opened a side panel on the droid and pushed some buttons. He told us he'd had the robot reprogrammed. The digital surveillance of what was going on at the Mint was encrypted and downloaded on him before the men slipped into his apartment.

"That's brilliant!" I said with awe. "Just like in the movie."

Roy shrugged, and then winced when his leg moved.

"Acupuncture will help."

"Needles? I don't think so, Rachel." Roy rearranged the covers, and I noticed he wasn't wearing a wedding band. It wouldn't hurt to get some more good karma.

"Hey Roy, are you dating anyone?"

He glanced at Ed before replying, "No," cautiously.

"Why not?"

"I haven't met anyone," he said.

"Want me to fix you up? I know lots of people. What are you looking for?"

Roy glanced at Ed. "Hey, don't look at me. She's in love so she wants the whole world to be," Ed said, grinning.

"Rachel, I'm injured. Have pity."

"Exactly, that's why you need love in your life." As soon as I said it, an image of the willowy K Bixler came to mind. "I have just the woman for you."

"Terrific," Roy said, and sighed.

• • •

Several things happened over the next few months. Uncle Pete aired Roy's Mint surveillance tape, and folks wanted answers. Politicians cloaked themselves in indignation and demanded action. A special committee to look into what was going on at the Mint was created. How had this been able to occur? Conspiracy theorists ran amuck, and the media started investigating the disappearing Dillinghams.

Interestingly, eight months after we'd filed our lawsuit to declare the government's automatic gag order in Qui tam actions unconstitutional, John Doe's hearing finally arrived. The judge waited thirty days to issue his ruling: a twenty-three page decision explaining why he was dismissing our case. I was appalled, yet understood the chess game we'd begun. The next step was a petition to the Unites States Court of Appeals. William's son Jason worked for a well-known civil liberties organization in Washington and was eager to take over the matter. In truth, it made sense. The nonprofit was better equipped to protect our rights.

And so life slowly returned to normal. Phil formally announced his return to the legal profession as news of Oliver's spontaneous awakening spread. His recovery was hailed as a miracle, and a party to celebrate was announced. Cheri Greene phoned to relay her warm wishes about Oliver, and we decided to meet Saturday afternoon at Marina's Café on Chestnut Street. She was a lawyer I'd spoken with when we'd first started the dead lawyer case, but had never met.

I felt someone's stare the moment I walked into Marina's Café. Turning, I looked into my eyes—again. "You," I said.

"Me," the lady with the green eyes confirmed.

We then followed a waiter to a table, and I soon learned we were both coffee addicts from Brooklyn. She felt so familiar. When I asked how she was able to hear me that day I was followed, she only said, "I just do. I suspect you do as well."

Shrugging, I invited her to Oliver's celebration.

More than fifty people showed up at Oliver's penthouse for the party. At one point I joined Phil and Arthur's conversation, and heard Arthur declare his love for a woman named Allison Khan. Tomorrow morning he was heading north to the wine country to surprise *his lady*. They'd e-mailed, then conversed on the telephone, and even exchanged a few letters.

"You met online? I'm surprised."

"It is the age of the Internet, young lady."

"So you've never met her?"

"Well, no. But I certainly know her. We've spent hours talking."

"But you've never met her," I repeated, looking at Phil.

"Not to worry. I can read your mind. She hasn't asked me for anything. In fact she sent me this beautiful cashmere sweater," Arthur said preening.

I wasn't mollified, but kept silent. He was happy, and I knew Phil would watch his back. So I wished him well and went to get another drink. From the bar I observed John and Cheri Greene. If one could see electricity connecting two people, you'd see it between them. As if sensing my stare, John looked up. I winked.

His barely perceptible nod said everything.

CHAPTER 29

I picked up Master Sun Tzu's pearls of wisdom and flipped to the back of the book. Grabbing a pen I added, "Deception and Perception are one and the same," and closed the volume. Kneeling, I slipped it back under our bed, just as Ed walked into the room and asked if I was ready. We were meeting John and Cheri Greene at Marina's Café for brunch.

The waiter showed us to an outdoor table, and I sat next to Ed. When Cheri started struggling to remove her sweater, John stood and helped her place it on the back of her chair, before returning to his seat. Looking across the table, I nearly fell off my chair.

Cheri Greene had a small tattoo—three interlocking infinity loops connected by a small slim oblong link above her heart.